"Sleep now," he whispered gently. *"We have a long, hot ride ahead in the morning."*

Beyond exhaustion, Faith did fall asleep, curled on the tarp under the blanket by the fire.

He looked down at Faith again.

"I don't know who you really are," he whispered. "But you're one hell of a woman, and I intend to find out."

She murmured in her sleep, and Omair felt a strange pang in his heart. God help him, he was falling, absurdly, for a woman sent to kill him, and it had started the moment he'd first laid eyes on her in that cantina on the banks of the Tagua River. And she *could* still be pulling the wool over his eyes.

Dear Reader,

Duty, honor, loyalty are traits that run fiercely through the blood of my Sahara Kings heroes. Above all, my sheiks stand for family, country and tradition, and they will fight to the death to protect those values and those they love. The hero of this story is probably the fiercest of all the Al Arif brothers. He's the lone rider, the dark horse prince, last in line to the throne, and the role of seeking justice for his family has fallen heavily on his shoulders.

But Omair Al Arif's values are tested when he unwittingly sleeps with his enemy—a woman with equal devotion to duty, honor, valor. She's a loyal soldier and an assassin, and she's given an order by her country to kill the man she's coming to love. Now both will be forced to choose between duty and obeying the heart.

I hope you enjoy their journey!

Loreth Anne White

LORETH
ANNE WHITE

Sheik's Revenge

ROMANTIC
SUSPENSE

Recycling programs
for this product may
not exist in your area.

ISBN-13: 978-0-373-27780-3

SHEIK'S REVENGE

LORETH ANNE WHITE

was born and raised in southern Africa, but now lives in Whistler, a ski resort in the moody British Columbia Coast Mountain range. It's a place of vast wilderness, larger-than-life characters, epic adventure and romance—the perfect place to escape reality. It's no wonder she was inspired to abandon a sixteen-year career as a journalist to escape into a world of romantic fiction filled with dangerous men and adventurous women.

When she's not writing you will find her long-distance running, biking or skiing on the trails and generally trying to avoid the bears—albeit not very successfully. She calls this work, because it's when the best ideas come.

For a peek into her world visit her website, www.lorethannewhite.com. She'd love to hear from you.

For Ola and Noor, who make the Sahara real.

Chapter 1

Sheik Omair Al Arif sat in a dark corner of the cantina, sipping the last of his espresso as he watched the woman working the bar. She was the single pleasure he'd been afforded over the past few months as he'd bided his time in this sweltering Colombian rathole along the banks of the Tagua River, watching, waiting, listening for a sign the deal was about to go down.

He'd positioned himself at a round wooden table in the shadows, his back to the wall—an assassin's habit. From this vantage point he could quietly watch the cantina door, as well as see who ventured in from a deck that tilted drunkenly over a coffee-colored estuary that snaked down through mangrove swamps to the sea.

Outside, monkeys screeched and swung from massive kapok trees that brooded over the building and sent giant roots down into the anaconda-infested waters. Inside, it was strangely empty for a Friday night.

An older couple, maybe in their seventies, drank beer from big mugs at a table across the room. At another table a group of men—cacao plantation workers—huddled over drinks and smoked dark tobacco cigarettes, skin glistening. Every now and then one of them would glance furtively toward the door. This was the heart of cartel country—life here was cheap, everyone on the take, and eyes were constantly shadowed with mistrust and fear.

Music played softly from an old jukebox in the corner.

The barmaid was wiping down the counter, her body gleaming with sweat. Omair could see from the way she moved that she was well aware of his appreciative gaze. Tonight she wore her bloodred dress, his favorite. The fabric flowed like liquid over her Latina curves and plunged down the front of her chest to expose a smooth olive-skinned cleavage, along with just a tease of black lace bra. He enjoyed the way her raven hair fell thickly across her cheekbones as she moved, the way she tossed it back over her shoulders, the way her deep brown eyes made him think of sex.

Her name was Liliana. The men who drank at her bar called her Lili, and they were clearly smitten by her sensual aura, her husky laugh, her easy smile. Omair had deduced she was the mistress of the cantina owner, a low-level cartel player himself, and that if any one of these bar patrons actually dared touch Liliana they'd be found floating facedown in the Tagua by sunrise. And no one would even blink.

It was that illicit quality, that promise of danger, that made Lili all the more enticing to Omair. Over the past months she'd become something of an obsession, a heady drug to his system.

Women were Omair's sole Dionysian weakness and one-night stands his specialty. His lifestyle did not accommodate anything more permanent. And when Omair did indulge he preferred his sex spiked with as much adrenaline and risk as possible because it made him feel truly alive for a few brief moments.

But Lili's delectable cleavage was decidedly off-limits—a fling with the Hispanic temptress would be a sure ticket to trouble with the local cartel, and that could blow his mission, a duty to which Omair was bound by blood, honor and a fierce code of ancient desert justice.

A mission he could not—*would not*—fail.

No, he was not here to mess in the business of the malignant cartel that controlled this region of the Colombian jungle. He was here to avenge the murder of his oldest brother, Da'ud, along with the assassinations of his mother and father, the king and queen of Al Na'Jar. Someone was trying to kill off the Al Arif bloodline and overthrow the kingdom. Omair's sole purpose in life right now was to hunt down and pick off those assassins one by one, then find the man who sent them, and kill him, too.

Only then would he go back to his job with a private army based off the west coast of Africa. Until that point he was a lone wolf, answerable to no one, and no thing, other than his ancient code of honor.

Already he'd meted out justice to two of Da'ud's assassins. Now he was after the third—the one who'd wielded the ceremonial dagger that had sliced his brother's neck to the spinal column as Da'ud slept on his yacht anchored off the beaches of Barcelona.

Before executing the first two men in Spain, Omair had forced them to yield information on the third man. He got more than he bargained for—he was told

Da'ud's third killer would be coming to Colombia as the bodyguard of a North African arms dealer to buy a cache of black market weapons from the Tagua cartel boss. The weapons were rumored to be of Chinese origin, just like the guns being supplied to rebels in Al Na'Jar. The deal was supposed to go down sometime this month, somewhere along this estuary. The truck-loads of arms were to be driven onto barges that would be floated down to the sea. The weapons would then be transferred to a ship waiting offshore and transported through the Panama Canal disguised as a cacao crop. From there the shipment was destined for the Western Sahara.

Omair's plan was to quietly and quickly capture, interrogate, then kill the North African's bodyguard. If he did it right, the man would simply go missing from the entourage as if snatched by a jaguar and dragged silently off into the dense surrounding jungle—it was not an unusual occurrence here. Time would continue to tick, and although the men might be put on edge by the disappearance of one of their hired guns, the weapons deal would by necessity still go through.

Omair would then track the arms shipment to the Sahara where he hoped to learn who was fronting the cash, hopefully getting closer to learning the identity of the man behind the coordinated attacks on his family and country.

Notice of the exact time and place of the weapons transaction was to be delivered to a contact in this riverside cantina, and it was why Omair had secured a job as a truck driver at a nearby plantation. It gave him an excuse to come into town daily for supplies. It gave him a reason to sit nightly at this table where he could watch and assess the locals, and wait for a hint of something big going down.

And he could watch Liliana. That was the bonus.

Lifting his cup to his lips he caught her gaze. She lowered her thick lashes and the corners of her full mouth tilted into a slow smile. Omair's blood heated.

She held his gaze for a long moment before easing her thick hair over her shoulder and returning her attention to a customer at the bar. She took the old man's order, reached for a bottle on the shelves behind her, then flashed another look at Omair. Her dark eyes sparkled as she leaned forward to pour the man's drink, affording Omair a clear view of the smooth delta between her breasts.

She was toying with him. It had become a game, and hot damn, he liked it.

Lili returned the bottle to the shelf and made for a door that led to the kitchen, her high heels giving a seductive sway to her walk. And as Omair watched the movement of her buttocks under the tight red fabric, his mouth went dry. She made him want. Dangerously so, because he couldn't—not this time. Not in this place.

As the kitchen door swung shut behind her, he breathed out slowly.

She was an enigma. Despite exuding a provocative sex appeal, Omair detected a quiet, calculating intelligence in Lili—a different kind of awareness. He'd glimpsed it when she thought no one was looking. While she appeared to feign disinterest in business talk at the tables, sometimes he'd catch her watching, or listening intently to her patrons, as if weighing, gauging, assessing them, like he was. Omair figured she was an opportunist looking for her next big step—or lay—up the cartel ladder. A more influential, wealthier cartel member would mean a big hacienda, more clothes, more opportunity for a woman like Lili.

He didn't hold this against her. It was likely her only ticket out of this Colombian cesspool. A body like hers was to die for. Be a shame not to use it.

Lili exited the kitchen carrying a plate of food. She set it on the table where the group of men huddled. They exchanged rapid-fire banter with her and she laughed, throwing her head back, the column of her neck gleaming in muted light.

The tinny music from the jukebox segued from a recent pop hit into the dramatic and strident chords of a Bolivian tango sextet. The mood in the room shifted.

The older couple got up, the man holding his hand out to his woman as he led her onto the tiny dance floor. They began to move in each other's arms, crumpled echoes of once strong individuals. The woman's sandals were dusty and had a broken strap. The man's pants were threadbare. A strange emotion caught Omair by the throat as he watched them dance to the sensual beat. It was an odd little vignette, a reminder of the endurance of love, the passage of time. Even in this dirty, dangerous little settlement that passed for a town in the heart of poverty-stricken jungle, the universal story of human love still played itself out.

That couple probably had been born here, grown up on the banks of the coffee-colored river, met, fallen in love, married, had children. Grandchildren. And although faded and bowed by time, they still had each other. In their minds they were still the same. They still had tenderness, compassion, love.

Like his parents once had.

Like his brothers Zakir and Tariq now had.

Omair swallowed the last bitter grounds of his

espresso, a chill crawling into his veins, and his jaw steeled. So did his heart.

This was his lot, his solitude. His warrior's duty to his ancient kingdom was now the pattern that shaped his days. No matter where in the world it took him, he was duty bound until justice was done, an eye for an eye, the old way. Omair wondered what would be left of him when it was over—a hollow husk of a killer incapable of love? A man forever denied what that old couple had?

But before he could dwell on the thought, Omair sensed a shift. The air around him seemed to thicken and his assassin's instincts prickled down the back of his neck.

He caught the scent of pipe smoke coming from somewhere out on the deck, the tobacco pungent. He heard the soft hiss of a feral cat and a small splash in the water. Omair slowly moved to touch the hilt of the dagger in his boot, and he felt the reassuring pressure of the pistol tucked at the small of his back.

A man entered from the deck, the heels of his snake-skin shoes clumping onto the worn wood floor. The aroma of tobacco smoke and cologne wafted in with him. He wore crisp dress pants, a pale yellow golf shirt open at the neck. A gold chain nestled in dark chest hair, and a fat ring embedded with a blue stone adorned his pinkie finger. His skin glistened with humidity. His black hair had been slicked off his brow with oil, accentuating a sharp widow's peak.

The group of men at the table fell silent. One by one they got up and began to leave as the stranger slowly crossed the scuffed floor. As he reached the bar the elderly couple scurried out of the cantina behind him.

Omair was now the only patron left in the pub.

He reached for his straw hat and tilted the brim over his eyes as he slid slowly back into his chair, feigning drunken sleep. Through the small holes in the straw weave he watched Lili offer the man a full-wattage smile. Omair was now certain—this stranger was high-level cartel and Lili was one hundred percent on the make. An inexplicable twinge of jealousy shot through him.

Without uttering a word, Lili reached for a bottle of the cantina's finest scotch. She sloshed three fingers into a glass and pushed it toward the stranger.

The man swigged it back, nodded for a refill. Lili poured again but this time, as she gave him the glass, she allowed the backs of her fingers to caress the man's hand.

The man withdrew his hand, tossed back his second drink, set the glass onto the counter, then turned abruptly and strode toward the exit.

Frowning inwardly, Omair remained motionless as the man passed his table. The man stilled for a moment beside Omair, then left as suddenly he'd come, via the deck.

A monkey screeched outside, shattering the silence in the cantina.

Slowly, Omair returned his attention to Lili.

She was peering into the rust-pocked mirror behind the rows of bottles, reapplying bloodred lipstick from a tube she kept behind the counter. Although her back was to him, Omair could just make out part of her reflection, and while her right hand was applying color to her full lips, her left hand was sliding what looked like a scrap of white paper into her bra.

His pulse kicked. *This was it.* His sign had finally come, and it had gone straight down that decidedly off-limits cleavage. He'd misread Liliana. She was not simply looking to sleep her way up the cartel ladder— she was a pivotal player, and Omair was convinced the time and place of weapons exchange was written on that piece of paper. He needed to get his hands on that note, stat, before she passed it on to someone else.

Seducing the barmaid had just become part of his mission.

From her view in the mirror Faith saw the tall, dark man rise from his chair in the far corner of the cantina. She quickly capped her lipstick and smoothed her dress over her hips before turning to offer him a big, warm smile. But her pulse quickened at the look of predatory intent in his oil-black eyes, the sense of purpose in the set of his jaw.

The jukebox had gone silent and the bar was empty. She reminded herself the bottles were weapons if she needed them—she'd once killed a man with a jagged shard of broken glass. She'd do it again if she had to. But in spite of her trepidation, a sharp, sensual aware-ness spiked into her system. She allowed her gaze to dip over him as he neared.

His jeans were faded in places that made a woman think of sin. The sleeves of his denim shirt were rolled up over darkly tanned, muscled forearms, and the shirt hung open to his waist, exposing washboard abs. His hair was black as pitch, his eyes hooded. His nose was aquiline, his features aggressive.

Part of Faith's assignment in Tagua was to identify key cartel players. She'd learned this man who'd been watching her from the dark corner of the bar for the last two months went by the name of Santiago Cabrero, and that he worked as a driver and laborer for a nearby cacao plantation. But he was not part of the Tagua cartel, and thus not part of her mission. Faith figured he was on the run, hiding some dark past, possibly a transgression of the law in some faraway place. Why else would someone choose to come to a place like this?

Faith could relate to keeping secrets—her whole life was one carefully constructed lie upon another, one alias after the next. She'd been faking it so long now she was beginning to forget who Faith Sinclair really was, deep down inside.

But irrespective of what dark secret Santiago might be harboring, his nightly vigil from the table in the corner had become Faith's sensual pleasure, a way to while away the long, humid hours behind the bar as she waited for notice of the hit. She'd begun to watch the clock each evening, anticipating his arrival. And he'd begun to invade her dreams as she tossed and turned nights under the mosquito netting in her bed upstairs. But he'd never made a move.

Until now.

Santiago splayed his hands on the counter, leaned forward, his obsidian eyes boring into her. Faith felt her cheeks heat as he seemed to pull her into his dark aura. At the same time she became acutely aware of all the exits, of escape.

"Another espresso?" she said quietly, in the local Spanish dialect, as always, cognizant of the bug the cantina owner had placed under the bar counter on behalf of the cartel. The listening device was the reason her contact had delivered the time and place of her hit via paper and not words.

"Tequila," he said.

A stillness went through Faith.

Santiago never drank alcohol—at least not in her bar.

"You celebrating something tonight?" she asked calmly, her pulse hammering as she reached for a bottle on the shelf behind her.

"No." He jerked his head toward a higher-end brand along the shelf. "Not that bottle—the other one."

Faith took down the more expensive bottle, opened it in silence and filled a shot glass. She slid it toward him, her eyes watching his.

Santiago swigged his drink back, slammed the glass onto the counter.

"Another," he demanded. "And pour one for yourself."

She smiled. "I don't drink on the job."

But he did not return her smile, and a cool thread of warning snaked through her.

"I've seen you drink near closing time, Lili," he whispered, touching her arm and softly tracing the backs of his fingers across her skin. Goose bumps shivered in the wake of his touch.

"The owner of this cantina," he said quietly. "Do you love him?"

She swallowed at the brashness of his question. Clearing her throat, she said, "He's good to me."

"How good, Lili?" He brought his mouth close to hers. She could feel the warmth of his breath against her lips.

"He gives me a job, a place to stay." Her voice came out thick.

"And he's good in bed?"

Heat pooled low in her belly, and her vision began to narrow. "He's fine."

He brought his mouth closer, and whispered, "I'm better. I want you, Lili. I know you want me, too—

I've seen how you look at me when I come each night to watch you."

She tried to smile again but the muscle in her lip quivered. Her breathing grew light.

"Your lover is away tonight," he whispered. "Isn't he?"

She'd wanted this, hadn't she—for Santiago to dare to attempt to seduce her? She'd wondered if he'd have the nerve to actually risk his life in an effort to sleep with her—none of the other men here would even think of trying. And the fact that he did was a dizzying aphrodisiac.

Faith reached for a glass, and poured herself a shot of tequila, buying time to allow some logic back into her brain. "Tell me about yourself, Santiago," she said, taking a sip. "Why are you in Tagua?"

His eyes darkened. A muscle pulsed under the dusky skin at his temple—he was exotic, a creature of masculine beauty and strength. And once she got out of this place, she'd never need see him again. Sleeping with him would be no threat to her—or would it?

"I'm here for a job," he said.

"On the plantation?"

"Sí."

"You running from something, Santiago?"

He smiled darkly, coming around to her side of the bar, and he cupped the back of her neck. Using his calloused thumb he tilted her face up to his. "Aren't we all?" His voice was low, gravelly, seductive. It curled like dangerous smoke through her mind.

"You're in trouble with the law somewhere, aren't you?"

His lips feathered ever so lightly over hers, his strong

hand holding her in place. "Does it matter where I left my troubles?" he murmured against her lips.

She swallowed, suddenly unable to think straight.

He slid his other hand down her waist as he spoke, down over her hip and around her rear. He caressed her butt and began slowly bunching her dress up her thigh.

Her vision blurred. She reached out for the bar counter, steadying herself. "This...could get you killed." Her voice came out hoarse.

"I know." He suddenly pressed his mouth down hard on hers. Faith's knees turned to jelly. She opened her mouth under his, felt his tongue, slick, hot, teasing the sensitive inner seam of her lips, and her world began to spiral into dizzying concentric circles, like a kaleidoscope, a fairground carousel, spinning. Faster and faster.

She tried to remind herself to be careful—a slip in her cover now could not only blow her mission, it could get *her* killed.

But she was tumbling over the edge of reason. Like a shot of heroin to her system, one touch, a few seductive whispers from Santiago, and she was hooked.

Loss of control was an unfamiliar feeling for Faith.

But what harm could it honestly do to take him to her bed upstairs?

He was right, the cantina owner was away. The bar was empty, no one to see. She'd be clear out of South America by tomorrow afternoon. By nightfall she'd be on a U.S. military jet bound for her Maryland base. The following morning she'd be back in her sterile Washington, D.C., apartment, biding time, trying to act out a normal life without ever really being allowed to, until STRIKE assigned her next hit. A government assassin's life was a lonely one. A cold one.

So what if she took fringe benefits every now and

then? It wasn't like she hadn't done it before. Anonymous sex was the safest kind of sex for a woman in her profession, and she hadn't been with a man in almost two years now. And the need in her was wild.

This is different, Faith. This man is not like the others—you don't have control...

He gave a small groan of pleasure against her mouth as his fingers found her G-string. He hooked his finger under the strap.

Lust ribboned through Faith like wildfire.

She reached up and threading her fingers into his thick, dark hair, she drew his mouth down harder against hers, her tongue seeking, tangling with his, her desire growing desperate. Against her hips she could feel the bulge in his jeans, and her body screamed—she needed him. All of him. Hard, fast.

But she had to get that piece of paper out of her bra first.

"Upstairs," she whispered, breathless against his lips. "I'll lock the doors."

Chapter 2

Faith woke with a start.

Parrots screeched in the branches outside her window and already the air was like a sauna. In raw panic she rolled over, groped around the bedside table, looking for her watch. A champagne glass clattered to the floor.

She jolted upright in her bed. For a brief moment she couldn't piece together where she'd left her watch, where she gotten undressed, what time she'd gone to bed. Then it hit her. Like a rocket. Her hand went to her forehead.

Santiago.

She must've fallen asleep in his arms. Her gaze darted around the tiny room that had been her operations base for the past six months. What time had he left?

Panic struck deeper.

She'd let herself go in the moment, during the best

sex of her life. She'd fallen into a deep, sated sleep in the arms of a stranger and she hadn't even noticed him leaving. How on earth could she have allowed that to happen, especially the evening before a major job?

Her gaze flashed to the empty champagne bottle and glasses. She recalled taking the champagne out of the small bar fridge in the corner of her room, thinking she'd secretly toast the end of her stay in Tagua. Sex with Santiago was her reward for hanging in.

Faith angrily threw back the mosquito net and lurched out of bed. As she got to her feet, a crushed white bloom with pink stamens fell from her hair to the floor.

Faith stared at the bruised petals near her toes.

Her attention shot back to her bed. Another bloom, this one perfectly intact, rested on her pillow. A mix of alarm and confusion spiraled through Faith.

Slowly, she reached for the flower. The petals felt like silk against her skin and a strange sensation tightened her chest. They reminded her of the white roses her mother had given her on her twelfth birthday. It was the first time Faith had ever been given flowers. It was the same day her mother had just given up and died, leaving Faith to face her father alone.

It was also the year Faith had first run away, promising herself she'd never be weak, like her mom; that she'd never allow a man to beat her into submission without fighting back; that she'd never bring kids of her own into this world, or dream about stupid idealistic lives behind white picket fences where families all smiled in church every Sunday, because she knew it was a lie. Behind the smiling faces hid drunks, wife beaters, bad mothers, bullies and cheats. She'd vowed to show her father a woman could not only be as strong as a man, but better. She was going to show her bullying father that she could be a real hero. Not a sham like he'd been—a man who wore his war medals on his chest and beat his weak wife in the secrecy of his home.

A tear slid down her cheek. Startled, Faith brushed it away.

In a moment of inexplicable panic she tossed the flower onto the pile of tangled sheets and moved quickly to her bathroom. She braced her hand against the bathroom wall, steadying herself as a wave of dizziness swept over her. She was still suffering the aftereffects of a stomach bug she'd contracted a week ago—she hadn't been able to keep food down for days and it had weakened her defenses, that's all this was. It had nothing to do with Santiago, or that flower.

Or her past.

Or the fact she'd lost control.

Faith's self-control defined her—it was the reason she'd become a top female sniper in the U.S. Army. It was why STRIKE had chosen to groom her as a NOC—nonofficial cover operative—for their deep black ops assassin program. She couldn't afford to lose it.

Faith quickly located her watch beside the sink and cursed when she saw the time. She had less than ninety minutes to get into position before the weapons exchange went down. She turned to reach for her clothes and caught sight of her black bra folded neatly on the laundry basket. Sweat broke out over her body—that wasn't how she'd left it.

She could swear she'd tossed it to the floor after quickly extracting and hiding the note hidden inside. Her pulse began to race.

Dropping to her haunches, Faith ran her fingers along the wall behind the toilet plumbing. She touched paper.

Relief washed through her as she extracted the note from where she'd stashed it behind the pipe.

For a horrifying moment she'd feared Santiago might have seen her slipping it into her bra earlier, and that he'd only made a move on her because of it. Faith dragged both hands over her hair and tried to calm her paranoia.

Okay, so she'd fallen for him, inexplicably, hard and fast. And she'd been a complete idiot to take him to bed. But it was done, over. He was gone, and she was never going to see him again. She'd treat it as a little warning sign for next time, but right now she had to think fast, get her brain into gear, steady her mind and her hands before she looked down that sniper's scope. Because her mission had been made crystal clear—hit *only* Escudero, the Tagua cartel leader. Collateral damage was to be avoided at all cost. This was in both U.S. and the Colombian government's interests.

Pablo Escudero was a drug lord turned international black-market arms dealer and a pain in the collective Colombian government butt. And not only had he made huge inroads into the U.S. gang underground, he was now aligning himself with known terrorist groups, as was evident by this latest deal about to go down. U.S. intel was that Escudero's cache of Chinese arms was destined for the Western Sahara where the guns would find their way into the hands of the Maghreb Moors—MagMo—a terrorist organization now rivaling al Qaeda.

Faith was to make her hit on Escudero appear as though it came internally from a rival cartel member. And she was to ensure the North African arms broker was not touched—the arms were to continue to North Africa. The CIA operative who'd delivered the details of the exchange was deep undercover in the cartel and he'd tagged the weapons shipment with GPS tracers. The CIA would follow the shipment to the buyers in the Sahara in the hopes of closing in on a key MagMo cell.

Sucking air deep into her lungs, Faith went to her fridge, took out a bottle of cold water and downed the contents. Then she removed her brown contacts and stared at herself in the mirror. Soft amber eyes stared back.

What happened to you last night, Faith?

Her pulse skittered with anxiety, but she tamped it down, quickly showered, tied back her hair, dressed for her mission. Packing only the bare basics, she then pried up the floorboards under which she'd stored the high-tech tools of her trade.

Pausing at the door, weapons bag in hand, Faith scanned the tiny apartment that had been her operations base—her home—for the past six months. It was the last time she'd see this hovel, or use this particular alias.

Goodbye, Liliana Rodriguez.

Quietly pulling the door shut, Faith sneaked down the back stairs. But as she donned her aviator shades and slipped down the jungle path, a sweet, heady scent snared her attention. She stopped, looked up at thick white flowers growing in a creeper that strangled around the trunk of a tree—the same blooms that had been left on her pillow. And in that moment Faith knew that while she could easily leave Lili Rodriguez behind, this time there was one thing she'd not be able to excise from her mind—Santiago Cabrero. And the small chink he'd made in her armor.

Hurrying along the jungle path, she told herself it meant nothing in the bigger picture. It was just a warning, and she'd heeded it. But a tiny niggle deep down told her different.

And that made her vulnerable.

Faith could not afford vulnerability.

STRIKE couldn't afford it.

She hoped it wasn't too late to pull herself together.

By noon Omair was in position at a little wooden table outside a ramshackle café about seven miles down river from the cantina, straw hat tipped low over his eyes, his legs crossed lazily out in front of him, one ankle over the other. Flies buzzed around the rim of a glass of flat cola, ice long melted.

Lili's note had said the exchange would go down across the street from this café shortly after noon.

A hot breeze rustled pieces of litter down the street and made a swishing sound high in the tops of thickly leafed trees. Above the jungle canopy, heavy clouds hung low in the sky and an electrical energy crackled in the oppressive air—felt like a storm coming.

Omair checked his watch. It was one minute past noon.

A cat skittered into a hole under the building, spooked by a cur trotting down the road with something unidentifiable in its mouth. Chickens pecked at crumbs under Omair's table. A pearl of sweat trailed slowly down the side of his face.

Omair focused on the tickling sensation of the sweat against his skin—anything to stop the smoldering images of Lili's naked body, the smooth feel of her inner thighs straddling his hips, the scent of perfume in her hair, the taste of her mouth…how she'd cried out and thrown her head back as she'd climaxed on top of him, the sensation of her sleeping naked and soft in his arms.

Omair inhaled deeply.

He'd lost focus with Lili last night and he could not allow the tantalizing memory to distract him further. He forced his concentration to cataloging his surroundings.

One side of the café was open to the air and inside a woman with large brown arms slowly wiped down a chipped counter. Behind her a television set was mounted on the wall. It was tuned to the CNB global news channel, volume cranked loud. Omair listened to the news, trying—and failing—not to think of Liliana.

Sex with her had been mind-blowing, combative, dangerous, just the way he craved it. But as the clock had ticked down toward dawn, Lili had remained alert and Omair had begun to worry he might have to resort to another method of obtaining the information on the scrap of paper she'd hidden in her bathroom. He'd also begun to fear someone might show up for the note and he didn't want to be there when they did. But finally her body had softened in his arms and she'd fallen asleep, head against his chest, her breaths deep and relaxed. Only then had he been able to extricate himself from her embrace and sneak into her bathroom.

Her bra had been lying on the bathroom floor, no note in sight. Omair had searched the bathroom systematically, thinking she had to have hidden it in there, because when she'd come out into the bedroom she'd been buck naked, save for her heels, and he was certain there'd been nothing in her hands. Finally he located the folded piece of paper behind the toilet plumbing. He read it carefully, and replaced it just as meticulously.

But he'd been distracted by his feelings about Lili, and he'd left the bra folded atop the laundry basket instead of tossing it back on the floor. It was a disturbing error, and a most unusual one for him.

Even more disturbing—on a much deeper and more personal level—were his complex reactions to Lili. Part of him had wanted to be there when she woke in the morning, to share breakfast with her, to find out more about who she really was. To hear her infectious laugh again. To see her smiling dark brown eyes.

Which was ridiculous.

And in a spate of foolishness he'd actually returned to her room to leave her flowers. He cursed inwardly.

She'd looked so beautiful, almost vulnerable, sleeping naked under that mosquito net that for a moment guilt had bitten into him.

Omair felt a hot rush of something akin to embarrassment at the thought of it. He argued with himself that leaving flowers had nothing to do with his guilt. Lili clearly brokered in sex. She'd wanted him as much as he her. The flowers were simply a way of saying thanks for the hottest damn night of his life.... Hell, he didn't know *what* they said—*that's* what ate at him right now.

He just hoped his slip with the bra was not going to somehow cost him this mission.

Faith lay flat on her stomach on a rocky knoll about a mile out from the small café. The jungle heat beat down on her, and in the distance thunder rumbled. Wiping sweat from her eyes with the back her wrist, she checked her watch, then put her eye to her long-range rifle scope.

Carefully she panned over the scene below, saw a man lounging at a table outside the café, feet stretched out in front of him.

Santiago?

Her pulse began to race as she scanned over the entire area again. This time Faith picked out Santiago's rusty truck parked deep in the shadows behind a thick nut tree. A chill washed over her skin.

He had to have found her note—why else would he be here?

Then she swore violently under her breath. He *had* wanted her for something other than her body and she'd gone and fallen for it like some pathetic ingenue.

But why—who did he work for? Had her mission been compromised?

Before Faith could think further, a plume of red dust rose above the distant trees, heralding the arrival of the weapons truck. Clearing her mind, Faith slowed her breathing and curled her finger softly around the trigger, waiting.

A black SUV emerged from the jungle, followed by a white Mercedes sedan and two trucks covered with military canvas. Another SUV brought up the rear. The convoy came to a halt on the side of the packed-dirt road, kitty-corner from the café. Three seconds ticked by.

Two jeeps appeared, coming from the direction of the river. They stopped under the trees a short distance away, facing the truck convoy.

The door of the Mercedes swung open. Escudero, the big drug lord, got out and straightened the jacket of his pale pink suit. Two bodyguards in dark glasses rushed around to flank him. More men got out of the SUVs. They carried submachine guns.

Faith positioned her crosshairs carefully over Escudero's face and her high-precision rifle showed an instant biometrics match. *Bingo*. She breathed in deep, then slowly out, and on the last of her exhalation, began to apply pressure to the trigger.

Through the weave in his straw hat, Omair watched Escudero and his close protection detail walk toward the jeeps. As they neared, a very tall and dark-skinned man alighted from the first jeep. Omair pegged him for the North African arms broker. The bodyguard to his immediate right turned to look at the café.

Omair recognized him instantly.

Da'ud's killer.

His body went dead still. He became aware of every sound, the slightest of movements, even in his peripheral vision...the café owner still languidly wiping down the chipped counter, the chickens pecking under tables, the Spanish news on the television set, the omnipresent hum of beetles in trees above him. Suddenly the voice of the CNB anchor cut into the newscast to say there was breaking news out of New York—a private jet taking off from JFK International had just exploded on the runway.

A chill washed through Omair's veins.

His brothers and sister were flying out of New York on the Al Arif jet today.

Zakir, the new king of Al Na'jar, had been in the city for a United Nations address. Tariq, a neurosurgeon in the States, and his fiancée, Julie, were to join Zakir and the royal entourage for the return trip to Al Na'jar for a holiday. Dalilah, their sister, was going, too—she wanted to be there when Nikki and Zakir's twins were born, and they were due soon.

Zakir had met Nikki, a doctor and volunteer aid worker on the run from her murderous ex-husband, after Nikki had inadvertently crossed into Al Na'jar with a band of war orphans she'd been trying to save. Nikki had been a godsend to his brother, because Zakir, at the time, had been struggling to cope with his new duty as king while trying to hide the fact he was going blind.

Nikki had helped Zakir through the process and in turn Zakir had helped her save the orphans. He'd married her, and given her a new life and identity. Nikki had become the guiding light in Zakir's new world of darkness. And now she was expecting twins. A great joy to them all because Nikki's ex had caused the death of their children, also twins.

Omair struggled to keep focus on his target approaching Escudero, but at the same time he was unable to tear his attention away from the violent images flashing on the television screen—flames, roiling black smoke, emergency vehicles, people running. He could hear sirens, screams. The camera flashed to a blonde reporter who said it had just been confirmed that it was King Zakir Al Arif's royal jet that had exploded right before takeoff.

Omair's throat closed as he was blinded for a moment.

"We're still awaiting confirmation as to who was on board at the time," said the reporter, pressing her hand to her earpiece. "There is no word yet about what caused the explosion or whether anyone could have survived. We will continue to bring you updates as the story unfolds—"

His two remaining brothers, his sister. Likely dead.

For a second Omair was rendered immobile. Time stretched.

Escudero was extending his hand toward the approaching North African. Da'ud's killer was standing back slightly, a smile on his face. And Omair's brain

suddenly snapped, rage mushrooming through his chest
as he exploded up from his chair. His hands went for
the automatic pistols at his hips.

Feeling as though he was moving in slow motion,
Omair extracted his pistols and began to stride toward
the group of men across the street, images of the plane
explosion searing through his brain, burning into his
eyes, consuming his logic. He raised his automatic
weapons, one in each hand. The bodyguards saw him
coming, tensed, spun around, lifting their guns. Someone yelled. One of Escudero's bodyguards lunged forward to push Escudero to the ground.

But before the man's hand could reach Escudero's
shoulders, before Omair could shoot, the top of the drug
lord's skull suddenly blew off in a fine froth of pink
that spattered into the North African's face and onto
the front of his shirt.

Everyone froze.

Escudero's body crumpled slowly down to the dirt,
and then flopped forward.

Silence hung thick.

The men suddenly started yelling, shooting at each
other in confusion as they scattered for cover from both
Omair and the hidden sniper. Omair began to fire. The
woman in the café started screaming as bullets blew
through her walls, shattering her television set and rows
of glasses. A flock of parakeets erupted from a tree in
a flurry of red and green feathers as they took off in
flight.

Da'ud's killer froze dead in his tracks as he saw
Omair coming directly for him.

The man raised his weapon and fired a burst of
bullets. They buzzed like hot hornets past Omair's
head. But Omair kept marching forward, covering his

progress by pressing the triggers on his automatic pistols, the recoil jerking like jackhammers through his body as men scattered in his wake. Omair wanted his target alive, for starters.

The North African arms broker raced for his jeep. Da'ud's killer, out of ammunition now, dropped his gun and fled after the North African.

Ferocity and purpose burned through Omair. He would *not* let his brother's killer escape, no matter the collateral damage, no matter the cost to himself.

One of Omair's bullets hit his target's hand. The man stalled for a second as blood began to darken the soil at his feet. In that time the North African yanked open the driver's door of the jeep, scrambled behind the wheel, reached for the ignition and hit the gas. Tires spun, kicking up red dirt as the jeep raced off, door open, leaving the bodyguard defenseless.

Omair holstered one of his pistols while aiming the other at Da'ud's assassin's forehead. As he reached the man, Omair unsheathed his ceremonial jambiya—an ancient weapon carried by his warrior forebears. Only with this dagger could he mete justice as per the desert code—an eye for an eye, a ceremonial dagger for a ceremonial dagger. Just like the blade that had killed his brother.

Panic burned in the assassin's eyes and his face dripped sweat as Omair grabbed him, dragging him into the dense jungle foliage and shoving him hard up against a tree.

"Please...don't kill me," the man pleaded in Arabic.

Omair had only contempt for the plea of this assassin who made a living killing others. As a broker of death himself, Omair believed an executioner should die

honorably when his time came at the hands of another—
and it always did come. That was the nature of this job.

"Is that what my brother said, when you came in the
night to slit his throat?" Omair whispered, pressing the
jambiya blade against the man's throat.

He could smell gasoline. He could hear more shooting, more yelling, men rushing into the jungle.

"Who paid you to kill Da'ud?"

The man squirmed, moaned, started to say something. But a crashing sounded in the forest undergrowth,
men coming toward them as they chased one another.

Tension strapped across Omair's chest. *"Tell me his
name!"*

But before Da'ud's killer could speak, shots were
fired through the thick leaves. A stray bullet hit Da'ud's
killer square in the throat. Blood and air gurgled and
sputtered from the wound. The man slumped into
Omair's arms. Hot blood soaked through Omair's shirt.

Omair checked the killer's pulse and swore violently.
He was gone, just seconds before he might have spilled
the name of the man who'd ordered him to assassinate
Da'ud.

Quickly, he lay the dead man's body on the ground
and rifled through his pockets, finding nothing. Then
he caught sight of a small medallion on a gold chain
around the man's neck. Omair lifted the medallion in
his fingers. It was the image of a sun superimposed
with a dagger.

The mark of the Sun Clan.

A chill washed through him.

The Sun Clan was an ancient tribe of warrior Moors
that had once ruled the Atlas Mountains in Western Sahara. They were rumored to have gone to battle with
the Al Arif Bedouins hundreds of years ago, clashing

over land that now formed the Kingdom of Al Na'Jar.
The ancient princes of the Sun Clan had this emblem
tattooed onto their skin. Omair frowned.

This was the first time he'd seen this ancient symbol in medallion form around the neck of a MagMo
terrorist. It troubled him—there appeared to be more
and more MagMo links to the unrest in Al Na'Jar, and
now this symbol tying back to an ancient battle with
the clan of his forebears.

He yanked the medallion loose, then pocketed it.
Crouching low behind thick ferns and leaves, Omair
listened for more sounds of the men in the forest. But
an explosion suddenly pounded the air, pressure thump-
ing against Omair's eardrums. He winced as a ball of
flames whooshed up from one of the weapons trucks.
Fire started to crackle into the forest.

Another explosion ripped through the air as the second truck went up. Through the leaves he could see Escudero's vehicles had also caught fire and the blaze was
spreading across the road. Black smoke roiled above
the forest canopy.

Cutting his losses, Omair slipped away into the jungle.

He'd lost his opportunity to get the name of Da'ud's
killer, or find out who'd sent him. He'd lost any chance
to follow the arms shipment—the weapons had gone
up in smoke. He might also have lost his entire family in the JFK jet blast, which would mean he was the
new king of Al Na'Jar—a role he did not want under
any circumstance.

Rage and grief seared fiercely through Omair as he
aimed directly for the distant knoll from whence he
believed the sniper fire had come. That sniper had just
cost him everything.

* * *

Faith watched in disbelief as the carnage unfolded in the distance.

Damn that bastard!

Santiago Cabrero—whoever in hell he really was—had single-handedly blown an international operation. He'd screwed up her hit, and Faith's handlers were going to have her head in a bag over this.

She'd never seen anyone handle automatic pistols like that. He'd walked into the fray as if on a death quest, denim shirt open to the waist, canvas bag slung across his chest, guns blazing. The fierceness of intent, the lethal focus she'd glimpsed in his oil-black eyes disturbed Faith on some fundamental level. What surprised her most, though, was that he'd seemed to go directly, and solely, after the bodyguard of the North African arms dealer. But whatever his mission was, he'd screwed up hers.

She rapidly dismantled her rifle, hurriedly placing the separate pieces of her weapon into her carrying case. Flicking the lock shut, she slung the heavy equipment over her shoulder. Faith threw one more glance toward the smoking fires before scrambling down the back of the knoll.

She'd seen the way Santiago had glanced toward her hide—she'd bet he was on his way right now.

But as Faith clambered in haste down the rocks, she slipped and her foot rammed into a crevice. Her body weight continued to carry forward, wrenching her ankle. She heard a pop and a searing pain shot up her leg. Faith sucked air in through clenched teeth, her eyes burning as she bent down to dislodge her foot. Her ponytail swung forward, tangling in the dead branches of a bush as she struggled to work herself free.

Once cleared of the rocks, she tried to put weight on her foot but gasped as pain roared up her leg again. Faith closed her eyes for a second, steadying her thoughts. Either her bone was broken or she'd torn a ligament. Which meant she wasn't going anywhere fast, at least, not until she splinted it.

A flock of birds burst from a tree nearby and she knew Santiago was close. In desperation she looked for somewhere, anywhere, to hide. Because she had no doubt that he was coming to kill her.

Chapter 3

Omair ascended the rocky knoll at a clip, shirt sopping with blood and perspiration, muscles burning. But his blind rage and anguish had finally honed down to a razor-fine focus, and his priority was rapidly shifting from finding the sniper to getting the hell out of Colombia before the cartel came after him.

The sniper was likely cartel, someone wanting to take leadership from Escudero. The hit on the drug lord probably had nothing to do with North Africans, or MagMo. And Omair's business was not with the cartel. Summiting the knoll, he quickly scanned the area.

This had to be where the sniper had fired from—it was the only place high enough with a vantage of the café in the distance. Omair walked to the edge of the knoll. He could see the burning trucks and smoke about a mile out. Whoever had fired the kill shot to Escudero's head was one hell of a sharpshooter, especially at this range. Liliana must have passed the note to the shooter.

Omair lowered his gaze to the flat slab of rock upon which the sniper had clearly rested. The shooter had made a hasty effort to dust over his tracks, but Omair could still make out marks left by a long-range rifle bipod. And he could see where the killer's boots had dug into the dirt, legs splayed. Omair frowned—the person who'd lain here appeared to have been slight.

He crouched down and touched the dusting of granular sand that covered the rock with his fingertips.

It was hot from the sun.

He traced the probable pattern of the body imprint, imagining the form of the shooter in his mind. With a little jolt he wondered if the sniper had been female.

Omair got to his feet and circled around the body print, cutting for a track. He found a footprint near the far edge of the knoll. He measured it against his boot and judged it to be a size seven shoe, narrow. More like a female's shoe.

Lili?

Then he shook the thought.

A glint under a bush caught his eye. Carefully moving leaves aside, Omair picked up a spent shell casing—a .50 caliber. He slipped it into his pocket. But as he was about to get up, he noticed a few strands of long, dark hair snagged on the bush and wafting softly in the hot storm breeze.

Thunder rumbled in the distance.

He untangled the strands and an image of Liliana brushing a thick fall of dark hair away from her face shimmered into his mind. His chest tightened. Could it be? Had the woman he'd slept with last night just

blown the top off Escudero's skull? Omair lurched to
his feet and swore.

He had *not* seen this one coming.

A toucan fluttered suddenly out of a tree to his left
and he spun around, raising his gun. Omair narrowed
his eyes as he scanned the surrounding jungle, gun leading. Nothing more moved, but he could feel a presence,
as if something was watching him....

Faith held her breath as Santiago scanned the foliage
around her. Sweat dripped from her brow and tickled
down between her breasts as she released the safety
on her backup 9mm Walther. She aimed it through the
leaves at Santiago as he peered into the branches.

She'd managed to drag herself up into the fork of a
massive kapok tree but the creeper she'd been holding
on to had snapped, spooking a toucan out of the upper
branches and almost sending her to the ground. It was
the toucan that had alerted him to her presence.

She clung now to a finer vine, the muscles in her left
arm burning, her ankle throbbing, her mouth bone-dry
as she trained her bead on Santiago.

He was close enough that she could clearly make
out his features, and his eyes were aggressive as they
scanned the forest. He stilled suddenly, as if sensing
something, and looked right at her. Faith curled her
finger around the trigger, heart thudding in her ears.

He took a small step forward, but stopped as if de-
ciding not to look for her further.

Faith slowly released her breath and pressure on the
trigger, then cursed when she saw he wasn't about to
leave yet. Instead, he was removing what looked like a
satellite phone from his belt. She wasn't sure she could
hold on much longer without slipping again.

He keyed the pad on his phone, put it to his ear, watchful of the surrounding jungle as he waited for an answer. He looked powerful, almost regal on the knoll. Faith wondered again what his motive was for going after that bodyguard and she bit into a sudden surge of self-recrimination—she'd been such a bloody idiot to have fallen for him like that.

This man was dangerous to her in ways that others weren't.

Facing in her direction, he spoke into his phone. And with a jolt Faith registered he was speaking Arabic.

Omair had expected a palace aide to answer Zakir's phone, so he was nearly blinded by a raw punch of emotion as he heard his brother's voice on the other end of the line.

"Zakir?" His own voice became hoarse. "You...were not on the plane?"

"I've been expecting your call, Omair." His brother's voice was tight, flat. "I cancelled my UN address because Nikki was having a few complications with the pregnancy. I sent an envoy instead. Dalilah came early to Al Na'Jar, on a commercial flight, also to be with Nikki."

"Tariq, Julie—they were on the plane?"

There was a long pause of silence. Omair's fist tightened on his phone. "*Tell* me Tariq is all right!"

Zakir inhaled deeply. "He's in a coma, Omair, in intensive care." Zakir fell silent again and Omair knew his brother was struggling to speak.

"How bad?"

"It's bad. He was flung clear of the plane in the initial blast, but he went back into the fire to save Julie. A second blast occurred as he was running with her from the wreckage. They were both badly burned. Tariq tried to revive Julie on scene, but she was gone. There was a third explosion, which flung debris that hit him across the head. He fell into a coma en route to the hospital. The doctors say it's from brain hemorrhaging. They've been working on him—"

"I'll fly immediately to—"

"No!" Zakir's forceful delivery brooked zero argument. "Do *not* go to New York. We don't know who did this. Our enemies are suddenly strong again—there's evidence of new cash flowing to MagMo, and if they are behind this, their resurgence could be because they have a new leader, a man who calls himself the New Moor. We don't know the extent of his reach and he could have people waiting for you to come to the hospital. You could be walking right into a trap, Omair, with Tariq as the bait. I want to bring Tariq here, back to Al Na'Jar, along with the best medical specialists available. When he arrives, I'll wait for a few days, then tell the world he has passed." Zakir paused, and Omair could visualize him, the blind king, standing beside the desk in his office, hand braced on the back of his chair for orientation and support.

"Does this work for you, Omair?" he said quietly.

Omair understood what his brother was saying. Tariq would be safer if their enemy thought he was dead. It also meant the enemy would now come directly for Omair. After Tariq, Omair was next in line of succession.

"Of course," he said, voice thick. "Have the doctors said what the long-term prognosis is?"

"If he does come out of the coma there will be extensive plastic surgery, a long haul to recovery." Zakir wavered, his voice going hoarse. "We need to be strong. For him, for our country, for our family."

Anguish twisted through Omair's chest and he reached for a rock to steady himself.

"Was it a bomb?"

"The U.S. Department of Homeland Security is heading up a joint task force to investigate. Our people are assisting. We'll know more as things progress. Where are you now?"

Omair steeled his jaw and took a deep breath.

"Da'ud's third assassin has now been eliminated," he said quietly. "I'm leaving Colombia for Ecuador—I know a pilot who'll take me tonight. From there I will fly to the Western Sahara. It's evident that the Maghreb Moors are behind this weapons deal, but I want proof. And I want the man calling the shots—if it's this New Moor, I want *him*. He could be spinning new ideology to fire his cause, using the ancient strife between the Sun Clan and the historic Al Arif Bedouin tribe to build identity for the MagMo organization, and if that's the case, it's going to hurt us because more might join their so-called cause."

"And that cause is?"

"To destroy us, the Al Arifs. And to take control of our kingdom, land they believe historically belongs to the Sun Clan."

Zakir was silent for another long moment, and when he spoke again, Omair could hear the grief and fatigue in his voice.

"Be careful, brother. I'll let you know as soon as anything develops with Tariq."

"We're going to win this battle, Zakir," he said quietly. "I will fight it to the end."

Omair killed the call and leaned on the rock.

He did not want to believe Tariq might not make it out of the coma, or that his brother might never be able to operate again. If Tariq survived and was not able to pursue the career, the passion that defined him, this alone would kill him. Not to mention how Tariq would feel when he woke to find Julie, the love of his life, gone, decimated by an unknown enemy.

Emotion burned fierce in Omair's eyes and his heart hardened with anger and pain. Heat shimmered in the humidity around him and the thunder growled closer. A few heavy drops of rain began to bomb the dry earth. The scent was strong. But everything seemed suddenly distant and the emotion in Omair's eyes turned into hot tears he could no longer hold back.

And as the tears leaked down the face of the assassin, he vowed to find and kill everyone responsible for this. It was his duty. He would go wherever in the world it took him, and he would not rest until he had justice for Tariq. An eye for an eye.

A life for a life.

Faith was fluent in Arabic—it was part of her training, but because of the noisy clatter of leaves in the mounting storm wind the only words she'd managed to identify in his phone conversation were bomb, MagMo, jet, explosion, Homeland Security and JFK.

Anxiety curled through her. If Santiago was a MagMo terrorist of some kind, and if it was found she'd slept with him *and* screwed up her hit because of it, she was as good as dead.

He was facing her now as he leaned back against a rock, and with shock she saw his features were twisted with raw emotion and tears glistened in his coal-black eyes.

Faith felt a startling reciprocal clutch of emotion in her chest at the sight of his pain.

What did he care so much about?

Faith hadn't allowed herself to care with that kind of passion or depth for anything or anyone for as long as she could remember. She curled her fingers tighter around the vine, her ankle throbbing, her muscles beginning to shake as she watched him. She was going to lose her grip if he didn't leave soon.

To Faith's relief, he pushed himself off the rock, glanced sharply one more time in her direction, then he disappeared down the opposite side of the knoll and slipped back into the jungle.

Clearly no longer his priority, Faith waited a few more moments to make sure he wasn't coming back. Rain fell more steadily as she slid carefully down the trunk of the tree. All she had to do now was find a way to splint her ankle and get to her evacuation point. Then she'd have to face the music over her botched mission when she returned to base in Maryland. Santiago might be gone for good, but her fling with him could very well have cost her her job. Possibly even her life. STRIKE was a fairly new and deep black ops outfit. Retirement of assassins from the unit was, as yet, an untested question.

All this because she'd been unable to resist those oil-black eyes, the smoke in his touch.

Washington, D.C. Late June.
Seven weeks after the Al Arif jet bombing.

Senator Sam Etherington, clear front-runner for his party's presidential nomination come fall, sipped his Earl Grey tea as he paged through the *Washington*

Daily. He stopped at the headline on page three—Dr. Tariq Al Arif, renowned neurosurgeon and geneticist, and next in line to the Al Na'Jar throne, had succumbed to his injuries and died at a private medical facility in the desert kingdom of Al Na'Jar.

As shoo-in for the presidency, terrorism and home-land security were cornerstones to his campaign, and so far there'd been no leads in the Al Arif jet bombing at JFK seven weeks ago. Nor had any group claimed responsibility.

Sam set his teacup carefully back into the saucer on his desk as he noted the byline on the story: Bella DiCaprio. She'd delved into the political ramifications of the surgeon sheik's death for Al Na'Jar. And in the stories following her initial coverage of the jet bomb-ing, DiCaprio had noted that the desert kingdom was recently oil-rich, and that there'd been ongoing unrest in the country, along with previous attempts on King Zakir Al Arif's life. The king's parents and older brother, she'd made a point of mentioning, also had been as-sassinated.

Sam committed her name to memory.

He liked to know the names of D.C. reporters, espe-cially the up-and-comers garnering big attention, and DiCaprio was one. Recognizing and calling reporters by name at media conferences had worked favorably for him to date—coverage tended to be more favorable.

A tap sounded on his office door.

"Come in!"

Isaiah Gold, Sam's special aide—a blunt political operative with an intelligence background—entered with an envelope in his hand.

Sam stilled at the look in Isaiah's features.

"We need to talk," Isaiah said, very softly.

Sam glanced at the envelope clutched in Isaiah's hand and folded his newspaper. "Take a seat."

Isaiah shook his head, and mouthed the word: *outside*.

Sam frowned. His office was swept for bugs and wiretaps once a week at Isaiah's insistence. Feeling a bite of tension, he reached for his jacket.

They sat on the wall of a fountain in the park across from Sam's office building where the noisy splash of water would obscure any attempts to record speech from a distance. The June sunshine was balmy and leaves fluttered in a soft breeze as Sam read the contents of the manila envelope. Then he read them again, anger swelling quietly inside him. He looked up, and met Isaiah's eyes.

"He can deliver everything it says in here—OPEC, Middle Eastern support, a major share of oil rights in Al Na'Jar?"

"If you uphold your end of the bargain and back the insurgency in Al Na'Jar, and if you help assassinate the remaining Al Arif royals."

Sam slapped the envelope onto the fountain wall. "There is no bargain! I don't know what has gotten into you, Isaiah. This man is incarcerated, being held in solitary confinement under U.S. military interrogation in Jordan! How in hell did he manage to get this proposition to you via an envoy anyway?"

"Sam," Isaiah said quietly with a placid smile, "you could still be photographed from a distance. Please, relax. Don't give anyone anything they can use against you. This is a critical time."

A tongue of panic licked through Sam. He glanced around quickly. A woman was walking a small dog at the far end of the park. Several sedans and a rusty white van were parked across the street. A couple walked hand in hand and a mother led her toddler over grass to the swings. Nothing unusual. But the information in the envelope was enough to make him paranoid.

"I'm going to pretend you never brought this to me." Sam said quietly as he stood up and calmly adjusted his jacket. Anger pounded in his head as he began to walk away.

"The proposal in that envelope doesn't come from the prisoner in custody, Sam. That old man is redundant to MagMo now. The organization has a new leader. This offer comes from him."

He swung back to face Isaiah. "What?"

Isaiah said nothing.

Sam returned to the fountain. "Who *is* this man?"

"We don't know," Isaiah said quietly. "He calls himself the New Moor. He appears to be well connected, and exceedingly powerful."

Isaiah opened his jacket as he spoke, removing a smaller envelope. "He sent this, too—a little gift, apparently, to sweeten his proposal."

Sam snatched the envelope from Isaiah, opened it. Blood drained from his head.

Slowly, very slowly, he sat back down on the fountain wall.

"Where did these photos come from?" His voice came out thick.

"Again, I don't know."

"Is it really her? *Alive?*"

"According to the New Moor's envoy, your ex-wife— the woman you had declared dead in absentia—is very much alive and thriving as the new, and very pregnant, Queen of Al Na'Jar."

"This...can't be."

"She always wears a veil in public, and she has not left the kingdom since the marriage. These photos were apparently taken inside the Al Arif palace." Isaiah paused. "The Queen's features are a biometric match to Dr. Alexis Etherington."

Nausea rose in Sam's throat. "You checked?"

"I had my man look into it, yes."

"You should have come to me first, before involving anyone else."

Isaiah's gaze was intense as he met Sam's, but there was a slight smile on his lips, in case anyone was watching.

"Sam," Isaiah said quietly. "This New Moor apparently has evidence that you hired a hit man to murder Alexis, but you ended up killing your five-year-old twins instead. Evidence, he says, that will hold up in court."

Hot fear roiled with nausea through Sam. He loosened his tie.

Isaiah was watching him intently. "Is this true, Sam—you tried to kill her?"

He said nothing.

"Damn it, Samuel, I can't cover for you, I can't spin things, if I don't know the facts to begin with!"

Sam moistened his lips. "What…what evidence does he have?"

Isaiah's keen, slate-blue eyes narrowed sharply. "I guess you'll find out when I tell his envoy you're not interested in his proposal. At best, the allegations alone could cost your bid for the party nomination. At worst, you'll be charged with homicide."

Sam sat silent for several beats.

"Are these so-called New Moor's people responsible for the jet bomb? Did MagMo kill Tariq Al Arif?"

"Yes. They'll be releasing a statement at some point in the near future." Isaiah leaned forward, resting his forearms on his thighs. "Consider this, Sam. If you help the New Moor, as proposed in that envelope, the Queen of Al Na'Jar—and your past connection to her—will die with her and her husband. The Moor will take control of the kingdom of Al Na'Jar, and you'll get unprecedented access to the country's considerable oil reserves, along with allies in the Middle East. These are campaign promises you can take to the bank."

"Why does this New Moor so desperately want Al Na'Jar?"

"Oil."

"That simple?"

"And that complex."

Sam sat silent, listening to the water splashing in fountain, unable to fully digest the fact that the wife he'd tried to get rid of all those years ago was coming back to haunt him now, in the worst way possible.

"Does King Zakir know who his wife really is?" Sam said, voice flat.

"Apparently so."

"Then why hasn't he acted, or used this against me?"

"He's protecting her anonymity. She's made a new life, wants nothing to do with her old one, even if it means letting you get away with murder, it seems. Bear in mind, she could face local charges, too—for fraud, obtaining false identification. She'd also potentially have to face you in court over the deaths of your children, which is something she'd probably prefer to avoid at this stage."

Rage boiled suddenly into Sam's veins.

"This knowledge makes that blind king dangerous!

He's a time bomb waiting to explode in my face—he could come after me years down the road, threaten the presidency, make demands." Sam dragged his hand over his hair, sweat dampening his body under his business suit.

"It's a bloody sword of Damocles." He spun to face Isaiah. "And this...New Moor...wants me to eliminate Sheik Omair Al Arif first, *before* the fall convention? In some kind of show of good faith that I'm on board with this proposal?"

"That is correct."

"Christ, Isaiah, how in hell am I supposed to do *that*?"

"You have unique access to a deep black ops assassin program at your disposal, Sam, a unit few even know exists—STRIKE. Use it."

"You've actually thought this through? You...you actually condone this."

"There's an operative they need to retire. An alarm was set off in STRIKE computers when a private forensics agency working on behalf of a private investigator tried to match her DNA profile in some major U.S. databases, which means her security has been compromised. The forensics agency is also in possession of a unique shell casing belonging to a one-of-a-kind prototype military sniper rifle—the kind *she* used for a hit in Colombia. There's a partial print on it. That partial print has also been run through key databases." Isaiah paused, allowing Sam to digest what he was saying.

"This operative needs to be eliminated, Sam, before the secrecy of STRIKE itself is compromised. Her name is Faith Sinclair. Use her. Let her take the fall for killing the Al Arif prince before she's eliminated in turn." Isaiah stood and put on his sunglasses.

"Once she's dead, your hands will be washed clean."

The engine of an old white van parked across the street from the park sputtered to life as the two men got up from the fountain wall and began walking across the grass toward Senator Sam Etherington's office building.

"You get anything, Scoob?" the stocky, dreadlocked driver said as he pulled into the traffic.

"Yeah, a whole crapload of fountain noise," said the pale technician in the back of the van as he fiddled with the connections to his homemade parabolic microphone. "Maybe I'll be able to filter out some of the background sound when I get my experimental system up and running."

"Yeah, maybe. *If* you ever get it up and running."

"Have faith, Hurley. Have faith."

Chapter 4

Washington, D.C. July.
Eight weeks after the Al Arif jet bombing.

Faith opened her safe deposit box inside the private viewing booth of her bank. She shouldn't be here. The cab was waiting outside, engine running. Her flight was due to depart the Maryland base in less than an hour. But she'd been unable to stop herself.

Taking a deep, steadying breath, she slowly removed a faded photo from an envelope in the box. It was an image of her mother holding Faith as a four-month-old baby on the base where they'd lived at the time. Faith was dressed in a white christening gown. Her father's large hand rested on her mother's shoulder—steering, controlling. The rest of her father's image had been torn from the snapshot.

Rage, pain, remorse surged inside her. Faith struggled to tamp it all down.

Usually it was easy to quash any emotions associated with her childhood, but since Tagua... She cursed, hating that she felt anything at all. She told herself it was just another damn symptom, along with the other changes that had been occurring in her body since she'd left Colombia—the increasing tenderness in her breasts, the nausea, fatigue, mood swings.

Faith quickly slid the photo into her briefcase, next to the pregnancy test she'd just purchased at the drugstore. She wasn't sure why she needed the photo now. It was the single personal item she'd kept from her past, as if one day she might need a window to revisit it. Hell alone knew—maybe she missed her mother.

Or maybe she was just terrified of becoming a mother herself.

Outside, the air was warm, trees in full leaf, grass green. Washington was pretty in the summer, and Faith looked like she belonged. Her hair had been returned to its natural blond and hung in a sleek ponytail down her back. She was dressed in casual business attire with neat heels, bare legs, a crisp blouse. But her skirt was tighter than it used to be, and dark sunglasses hid eyes that had seen too little sleep since she'd left Colombia.

For the duration of those eight weeks Faith had been held at a high security location on a Maryland military base used by STRIKE, and for the entire time she'd been worried she'd be scrubbed, that someone might have seen her with Santiago.

But late last night word had finally—and suddenly—come that she'd been cleared, and immediately she'd been handed a dossier for a new rush job in Algeria. She'd left at once for her apartment in D.C., packed her bags, and this morning she was back at work, and thankfully off crutches—the weeks of detention had given her torn ligament enough time to heal.

But time in detention had also left her zero opportunity to privately access a pregnancy test, until now. Heaven knew when she'd be able to use it in private— maybe when she reached the hotel in Algiers, right before the hit.

As she ran back to the idling cab, Faith tried to tell herself the test would come up negative, that the changes in her body were due to stress, a lack of exercise, or something—*anything*—else.

Because if she was carrying Santiago's baby—or whoever he really was—it would be the worst possible thing that could happen to her now, both professionally and personally.

Omair adjusted the collar of his linen jacket as he stepped out into the hotel courtyard and into the searing summer heat of an Algiers morning. For the past two months he'd been posing as a black-market weapons broker with stock to offload, hoping to flush out the buyer of the botched Tagua cache. And finally he had—a Russian who counted the Maghreb Moors among his top clients.

The Russian had invited Omair to breakfast with him at the historic hotel in hope of sealing a new deal for his clients. Omair's immediate goal was to find out just what kind of arms the MagMo were seeking, and for what purpose. And he wanted to know who was going to pay for the weapons.

The entire courtyard of the hotel had been reserved for their meeting and the Russian sat waiting for Omair at a table covered with white linen under the vines.

His bodyguards were on the other side of the wall, at Omair's request. The Russian rose to his feet as Omair approached.

He was a short man, but made up in breadth what he lacked in height. His skin was deeply tanned. Dark glasses hid his eyes, and his hair had been oiled back from a pocked brow. His white jacket was too tight and the lapel sported a red carnation.

Inwardly, Omair grimaced. In his opinion the Russians always lacked taste, and this man was no exception. Omair made his way toward him, extending his hand in greeting.

Faith positioned her rifle between the stone crenels of an ancient battlement and peered through her scope at the courtyard far below. She was lying on the hot rooftop of an old Moorish structure in the traditional Arab quarter of Algiers, a city founded over a thousand years ago and steeped in the history of its conquests. In the distance the Mediterranean sparkled dark blue over a vista of whitewashed buildings with faded ochre rooftops, and towering palms dotted the shoreline.

But all she could think about was the pregnancy test in her sling bag.

The stick had turned blue.

Sweat dribbled into her eyes. The heat was making her sick. Her stomach and swollen breasts felt uncomfortable pressed against the hot concrete rooftop. She swallowed a sudden surge of panic.

She'd dodged a bullet in being cleared after the botched Tagua hit, but now this pregnancy could mean her job anyway. Assassins couldn't just "quit"—the secrets she knew could bring down governments, start wars. Another sharp wave of nausea forced Faith to close her eyes for a brief instant. But the image of Santiago, naked, burned behind her lids. Her mouth turned dry.

You can't think about it now. The test might be false positive. Do another when you get back. And you don't have to keep the baby...just focus on your job...

Faith opened her eyes and peered through her scope again, forcing her attention back to the courtyard below. In her mind she replayed the notes from the dossier her handler had given her to study on the plane. This mission had been a rush one. No photo or biometrics indicators had been provided. All she knew was that her target—Faroud bin Ali—was a top terrorist with the MagMo and had so far eluded cameras. Her instructions were to watch for a CIA plant with a red carnation in the lapel of his white jacket. When the plant removed the carnation and set it on the table, it would mean her target had entered the courtyard and been positively identified.

Faith watched as the thickset man at the table under the vines stood up. He was reaching for the carnation in the lapel of his white jacket.

Adrenaline trilled softly through her blood.

The man removed the red flower and laid it next to his water glass. She controlled her breathing and her heart rate, curling her finger softly around the trigger as a tall, well-built man emerged from under the shadows of the vine trellis, black hair shimmering in sun.

Faroud bin Ali.

Faith carefully positioned the crosshairs over his head, breathed out, and on the last of her exhalation, she started to apply pressure to the trigger.

The man turned his head and shock slammed through her.

Santiago!

Her hands froze. Her heart jackhammered as thoughts skittered, tumbled, raced through her mind. The father of her baby—her target—a top MagMo terrorist? She was essentially a U.S. soldier. She had an order. She had to do this. Faith began to shake.

She told herself MagMo was endangering the lives of thousands of civilians. She *had* to follow her orders— she *had* to kill him.

Swallowing, she pulled the trigger.

But in her brief second of hesitation her target had moved a fraction to his left, and her slug exploded into the white plaster in the wall near his head.

He ducked sharply, spun around. She could see his black eyes, and he was staring right at her.

Faith quickly aimed again.

But he was too fast. He'd already grabbed the CIA operative around the neck and was using the man as a human shield, dragging him back under cover of the vines. Faith caught a glimpse of them through the vine leaves, and she saw her target slice a dagger across the operative's throat. Arterial blood spurted out, drenching the white suit.

"Santiago" dropped the man to the ground and ran toward the back wall of the courtyard. Faith tried to follow his movement under the vines, but as she drew another bead on him, something buzzed like a hornet past her ear and thwacked into concrete near her face. She gasped and jerked back as the concrete exploded into shards, one of them slicing across her brow.

She rolled onto her side, dropping about a yard down onto a ledge. She sucked in a burst of pain as her shoulder took the brunt of her fall.

Faith lay there, listening. Blood leaked into her eye.

Sun beat down hot. But all she heard was the noise of bullhorns coming from the market in the casbah, the sounds of traffic, horns, the chirps of tiny birds darting through clotheslines strung from windows in the building below.

Carefully, she peered back up over the parapet and caught sight of a tall figure in a white robe and dark red turban up on the balcony of a gold-domed minaret that towered over this area of the old Arabic quarter. What the hell—who was *that?* The man raised a rifle, and another shot zinged past her face as she ducked back.

Faith swore, waited a breath, then quickly belly crawled to the far end of the roof using the parapet as cover, thinking that in another few weeks she'd be unable to do this—if she kept the baby. She edged carefully up behind a stone merlon. The minaret balcony was now empty.

Faith dropped back. Panic licked through her stomach. But who in hell was that robed shooter in the minaret?

She didn't have time to think about it. The Algerian police could arrive at any minute and if they arrested her, STRIKE would cut her loose and she'd be left to rot in an Algerian prison.

Faith began to rapidly unscrew the components of her weapon, slotting the pieces into the holsters strapped to her legs and torso. Quickly tying a scarf over her nose and mouth, Faith then covered herself in the black chador she'd stuffed into a fake leather sling bag. Soft wire hoops had been sewn into the chador hem so the fabric would stand away from her body, hiding the angular weaponry strapped underneath.

Crouching with her back pressed against the hot stone, Faith used her sat phone to dial the number her handler, Travis Johnson, had given her for details of her extraction.

The phone rang, and rang, and rang, then cut off.

Another bullet suddenly pinged off the top of the merlon.

Her heart kicked.

The mystery shooter was still out there.

Bunching up the fabric of her chador, Faith crawled toward a doorway that led to a crumbling staircase down the outside of the building. She crouched at the top of the stairs, redialed the number. Sun baked down on the rooftop, the black fabric of her chador making her even hotter. Someone picked up. A recorded voice said this number was no longer in service.

A chill slaked through Faith.

She closed her eyes for a moment. If she couldn't reach anyone for an evac, she'd have to go to plan B and make it to a safe house along the outskirts of the sprawling Algiers metropolis. The route had been mapped into her GPS, and scored into her mind.

No more shots came from the tower. Faith edged up and, using her military scopes, carefully scanned the minaret balcony, then the stairwell that curled around the tower. She caught a movement, a glimpse of a dark red turban—the man was running down the stairs. Coming after her?

She quickly redialed the evac number thinking she might've made an error. Again, three rings, then the recorded message saying the number was not operational.

Faith swore and pocketed the phone in her sling bag. Gathering the ends of the chador in her hands, she ducked through the crumbling doorway and ran down the narrow stairs, planning to vanish into the crowded market in the ancient medina below.

* * *

Omair raced for the old building near the casbah where he'd seen sunlight glinting off metal along the ancient battlements atop the roof, dodging through traffic and bumping into pedestrians as he went. The shot had to have come from that direction—it was the perfect place to put a sniper. Anger boiled through Omair's veins—the Russian must have checked him out, seen through his cover, and tipped off an Algerian MagMo cell. Omair had been set up like a sitting duck in that courtyard.

There was no way in hell he was going to let that would-be assassin escape now. And when he got him, he was going to take his captive out into the desert and do whatever it took to make the bastard spit out the name of the man who'd ordered Omair—and his family—dead.

Omair swung into an empty alley and stilled, breathing hard, his shirt drenched. He glanced up and down the street to see if any of the Russian's bodyguards had managed to follow him into the maze of twisting alleys and stairways. The casbah was an ideal place to hide. It's where he expected the would-be assassin to come down from the roof.

A woman in a chador, dark sunglasses and veil, carrying a sling bag suddenly dashed out of a doorway ahead. She paused, glanced his way, froze as if startled, then spun and sprinted like an Olympic athlete down the alley and around a corner, gone, like a black ghost.

Omair gave chase. It had to be the sniper—it wouldn't be the first time a man had hidden under the veils and chador of a woman. He lurched around the corner, saw the shooter racing up a flight of uneven stone stairs that had sunk in the middle with years of use. The shooter stopped at the top, glanced his way, then ducked to the right down another narrow alley.

Omair charged up the stairs, lungs burning. He swung to his right, entering the alley, and ran slap-bang into a mule loaded with garbage. Trash clattered out the bags and a man with a stick yelled a string of Arabic curses. Omair tried to edge past the mule while avoiding the old garbage collector's swinging stick.

Another string of expletives followed him as he raced down more uneven stairs and into a wider cobblestone street. The noise of the market grew loud—vendors blaring the merits of their wares over loudspeakers, high-pitched music from ghetto blasters, people yelling in rapid-fire streams of Arabic. And Omair could smell the rich fragrance of spices, cooking meat, incense.

He entered the bustling market, carefully scanning the crowds. He was looking for something that stood out among the ordinary, something not quite right. Omair moved slowly, purposefully, silently, cutting through the crowd like a shark, people parting in a wake around him.

Suddenly, a black-robed woman carrying a sling bag caught his gaze. She looked heavyset by the way the chador stood out from her body, and she was moving slowly, but it was the shoes that alerted him—badass, dun-colored desert boots topped with gaiters. The other women in the market were all wearing sandals, mules, running shoes. Those boots meant business—and they were making for the far exit of the medina.

Omair ducked down a side alley and quickly circled around the back end of the market, approaching the exit from the outside. It was quiet in this section of the cas-bah, more derelict, more shaded from the sun. He could smell rotting garbage and cat urine. Omair ducked into a dark alcove and drew his dagger.

He heard his quarry approaching—a slight squeak from soles against the grit of sand that had blown in from the desert, the swish of fabric around pant legs.

The footsteps stopped suddenly.

Faith paused. She thought she'd seen a shadow moving farther up the alley. She stood dead still, listening as she peered into the gloom. It was dark here and the alley narrow. Plaster chunks had fallen from walls and garbage lay in alcoves. A tin clattered to her left and Faith whirled around. A stray cat fled across the cobblestones.

Faith almost laughed with relief. She leaned back against the wall for a moment, catching her breath and willing her heart to calm.

Her plan was to find her way out the back of the casbah, and then to the safe house where she was supposed to receive further instruction. Part of her was afraid to return home—she'd failed another hit and there would surely be consequences.

She'd also have to face her pregnancy.

Inhaling deeply, Faith began to move cautiously down into the dark, narrowing alley. But before she'd made even five yards, she felt a grip around her neck as someone slammed into her from behind.

She tried to gasp for air, but her assailant was strong, choking her. Faith's eyes watered as she rammed her elbow backward into her assailant's gut. But his stomach muscles were like iron and her efforts were futile as he dragged her kicking into a dark alcove. His grip around her neck was like a vise, and tightening. Her vision went red, then black, small pricks of light circling. She fumbled blindly for the knife hidden under the folds of her chador, but as she grasped the hilt, her attacker swung her around to face him and lifting her off her feet, he slammed her back against the wall. Air gushed from her chest as the knife released from her fingers, clattering down to the cobblestones along with her bag.

Gasping for breath, air once again filled her lungs and as her vision returned his face swam into focus. Faith's heart slammed against her rib cage—it was him, her target. Faroud Bin Ali. Santiago.

And the look on his face was murderous.

Faith kneed him hard in the groin. He grunted in pain, but as he doubled over slightly, Faith felt the tip of his dagger press into her stomach. She went dead still as she felt steel meet skin through the fabric of her clothes. And all she could think about was the tiny life growing inside her belly, and what harm the knife could do to it.

A raw primal urge to stay alive rose through her body, overriding everything else.

"Santiago," she whispered hoarsely in Spanish. "Please, don't do this."

His eyes narrowed sharply. He reached up, yanked the veil and glasses off her face, and tore the chador hood back from her hair.

Chapter 5

Shock ripped through Omair as he looked into soft amber eyes lined thickly with black kohl. Blond wisps escaped her French braid and blood dribbled down the side of her face from a gash across her temple.

But there was no mistake—it was her. The woman he'd not been able to excise from his mind or his heart since Tagua was right here in North Africa. And she'd just tried to blow his head off. Her leonine eyes held his, unflinchingly.

"Who in hell are you?" he growled, pressing the steel blade of his dagger against her throat. "What are you doing here?"

"Santiago, please, you don't want to do this. Put the knife down." This time she spoke in fluent, soft Arabic and for a nanosecond something inside him almost wavered.

"You just tried to kill me, *Liliana*," he growled though his teeth. "Why? Who sent you?"

"I don't know what you're talking about."

"Like hell you don't!" He spun her around again to face the wall as he lifted the hem of her chador. Underneath, pieces of a high-tech sniper rifle were strapped to her body. Omair drew his pistol, cocked it, and stepped back.

"Turn around, nice and slow. Hands out at your sides."

She did as he said.

"Take off the chador."

Her eyes tightened in defiance, two hot spots forming on her cheekbones.

"Do it!"

She yanked the robe up over her head, and dropped it to the ground where her sling bag and knife lay. Underneath she was wearing camouflage cargo pants, a lightweight cotton shirt, hiking boots, desert gaiters, and she had a handgun and military-style water pouch strapped to her hips in addition to the rifle components.

In spite of her gear, the weaponry, in spite of the defiance crackling in her eyes, there appeared something softer about her than he remembered. She seemed more feminine, her curves more generous—lush even. Maybe it was the blond hair, the color of her eyes that made her even more stunning.

Omair checked himself—she was a cool-hearted killer who knew just how to use her looks. He'd seen what she'd done to Escudero's skull, and she'd just tried to do the same to him.

"Take off the side piece and water pouch, drop them at your feet."

She unstrapped the pouch, mouth tight. She let it fall to the ground, followed by her gun.

"Now face the wall again, hands up, legs apart."

Again, she acquiesced. Omair had a sense she was quietly waiting for a gap. Well, he wasn't going to give her one. Or he'd be dead.

He unbuckled his belt, yanked it from his pants, stepped forward, and quickly grabbed her hands down from the wall. He bound them tightly behind her back using his belt.

He wrapped her veil over her nose and mouth, then scooped her chador off the ground, pulled it back over her shoulders and hair and secured the clasp at the front. Now she was bound and essentially trapped under the oppressive black fabric.

"Who sent you to shoot me, Lili?"

She remained silent, eyes defiant above her veil.

He pressed his body against hers, forcing her backward against the wall. "Either you'll tell me now, or later," he whispered, near her face. "And believe me, now will be easier."

She swallowed slightly, but her gaze never flinched. "I didn't shoot you. I missed."

He laughed.

"I never miss."

A slither of emotion went through him. "Why did you?"

She moistened her mouth. "I looked through my scope and saw it was you," she said quietly. "I hesitated, then lost my mark."

"Yet you still pulled the trigger," he said, knowing on some level she'd already hooked him again and was reeling him quietly in, or he would not even be having a conversation.

She remained silent, pulse at her neck throbbing.

"If you weren't expecting to see me in your cross-hairs, who did you think you'd come to shoot?"

She said nothing.

Irritation flared in Omair. "Damn you, Lili," he growled, his mouth close to hers, so close he could almost taste her, and God, he wanted to. Up close he could also catch the scent of her shampoo. In spite of himself he felt his body stir, and intrigue whispered through him.

"I fell for your act once, in Colombia," he said. "It's not going to happen again."

"I think you should let me go," she said coolly. "Before I scream for the police."

"Go ahead, scream."

This time her eyes watered.

"Right, maybe you don't want the Algerian police to see what you have strapped under that chador. Possibly you don't have the right papers to be here, even?"

Still holding his gun to her, Omair scooped up her knife and bag from where they'd fallen to the cobbles. He took a quick inventory of the purse contents—GPS, sat phone, and just as he thought, no ID documents. He dropped her knife and water pouch into her bag and slung the strap across his chest.

Removing the rifle components strapped to her body would have to wait until he had more time and privacy, but she wouldn't be able to assemble them under her chador with her hands tightly bound behind her back.

Holding his pistol inside the leather bag slung across his torso, he kept the snout aimed at her waist. With his free hand he grabbed her brusquely by the arm.

"Now, walk nicely with me," he whispered against her ear. "Make like you're my wife. Screw this up, *Lili,* and I'll shoot where it counts. You'll bleed out before anyone even knows you're hurt under that black robe."

She glowered at him over her scarf. He replaced her

shades, and led her down the alley, back toward the noise of the market.

"Where are you taking me?" she said with a calm that belied the tension he could feel in her body.

"Somewhere private." He bent down, bringing his mouth close to her veil, and he inhaled her scent in spite of himself. "Perhaps your employers didn't tell you, Liliana—if there's one thing I'm very good at, it's making people give me information. I never fail," he whispered. "Ever."

And then he'd kill her, Faith was sure of it.

The longer she kept silent, the longer she'd live, and the more opportunity she'd have to escape. Time was her weapon now. And if she thought about it logically, he'd just given her a second chance to finish the job she'd been sent to do—which was kill him.

She still had a chance to go back home with her head held high and her career intact.

As her captor marshaled her back into the mayhem of the market Faith scanned her surroundings for possible escape routes. At the same time she remained acutely aware of the pistol pressing into her waist from inside the bag—the bag that contained her positive pregnancy test. Faith hadn't wanted to leave the wand in the hotel room garbage can so she'd slipped it inside the lining of the black bag along with the photo of her mother.

She glanced up at the harsh, yet striking profile of her captor—Faroud bin Ali. She was carrying his child, the child of a notorious and wanted terrorist that she'd been sent to eliminate. The idea was surreal. But she couldn't dwell on her pregnancy now. Her priority was survival—and to finish her job.

He escorted her up to a stall where he began rapid-fire negotiations for the purchase of two robes and some bolts of cloth. All the while he kept the bag and pistol pressed into her side.

Faith listened to him, her brain racing to find avenues of escape as she continued scanning the marketplace crowds. At the same time she wondered why Faroud, a key MagMo terrorist, had been posing as Santiago Cabrero in Tagua, and why he'd wanted to scuttle an arms cache destined for MagMo. It didn't make sense, and it made her uneasy. Even more troubling was why STRIKE had tasked *her* with the hit on him. Was it possible they knew of her interaction with him in Colombia?

Had she been set up? How? Did the man in the minaret have anything to do with it—and what about the disconnected evacuation number? A chill slaked through her in spite of the heat. She reminded herself that STRIKE operatives functioned exclusively on a need-to-know basis. The unit was so tightly compartmentalized she didn't even know who the other operatives were, unless in the rare event she was assigned to work with one. There could be a rational explanation for this all, and she hoped she'd find it once she reached the safe house.

The Arab vendor packaged the garments and handed them to Faroud. He bundled them under his arm and led her into a throng of people jostling beside another stall.

"This way."

He held tightly onto her arm as he bartered for two goatskin water pouches, ropes, a sheet of canvas, blankets, a kettle, pot, rice. He also bought dates, nuts and tea. He was preparing for a trip.

Anxiety skittered through her—he was going to take her out into the Sahara, where she'd be out of her element. She needed to escape before that, but couldn't see how. Heat beat down, the noise and strong scents of the market making her dizzy and nauseous. Faith also felt thirst, but her captor had taken her water pouch. She considered asking him for it, but before she could think further, Faith caught sight of a tall man in white robe and dark red turban. He was moving with purpose through the crowd, directly toward her.

"That man," she whispered urgently to her captor. "He's going to try and kill me."

"What?"

"I said he's going to kill me."

"Why?"

"I don't know!" Panic licked. She was trapped, defenseless with her arms bound behind her back under her chador. The gun was still pressed into her side. All she could do was use Faroud, rely on his desire for information to keep her alive.

"He tried to shoot me from the minaret after I fired at you," she said. "Look, he's coming this way," she hissed under her breath. "You've *got* to let me go."

The man neared, but Faroud turned his face away, and continued bargaining for his purchases from the stall. Faith cursed him as the red turban came closer. Her heart began to race. She considered bolting, but Faroud's gun was still pressing into her waist. Then suddenly Faroud laughed loudly at something the vendor said, and he spun around, bumping sideways into the man with the red turban. The man stumbled, fell.

"Come," he said to Faith, gripping her arm.

She stared, incredulous, at the man lying on the ground. He wasn't moving. Blood was pooling under him. She glanced at her captor. His eyes were hard.

"I said *come.*"

He yanked her arm and propelled her quickly toward the large keyhole archway at the market entrance.

"Faster," he said quietly near her ear.

She glanced back over her shoulder. A crowd was starting to gather around the fallen man. A woman screamed.

Faith swallowed as her abductor led her quickly under the archway and out into the traffic-congested street. She hadn't even registered that he'd unsheathed his dagger and stuck it into that man's gut.

He was one frightening and skilled opponent, one she could admire—*if* she was on the same side.

Vehicles crawled along the road outside the casbah, exhaust fumes stinking hot. Her captor marched her toward a line of yellow taxis.

"Who was that man?" He spoke fast, eyes scanning the street as they walked.

"I don't know. Thank you for taking care of him."

He stopped, looked down into her eyes. His features were tight. "Who are you? Does life mean absolutely nothing to you?"

Faith reeled at the sudden judgment, at the anger in his eyes. This man was MagMo. He brokered in terror, the death of innocent civilians.

"You have no right to judge me!" she snapped. "I saw what you just did to that man back there, a man you didn't even know. I could have been lying to you, yet you killed him without blinking or breaking stride."

She glared at him. "What were you doing in Colombia anyway?"

"I had a purpose."

"*What* purpose?"

He shoved her toward a cab, opened the door. "This is my show. I ask the questions. Get in."

She scrambled in, her body humming with sudden rage. She wanted to yell at him that he'd screwed up her mission that day in Tagua, that he'd screwed up her entire life. And now she was carrying his baby. But the truth was she bore equal responsibility. She'd made the decision to sleep with him. She was the one who'd lost her mind over him.

Sitting awkwardly with hands bound behind her back and rifle components poking into her body, Faith clenched her teeth as Faroud climbed in beside her, his powerful frame dwarfing hers. He kept the pistol in the bag pointed at her as he instructed the driver to go to a place he referred to as the camel market.

His body was warm against hers. The heavy black chador and veil bound tightly over her nose didn't help with the heat, and there was no air-conditioning in the cab. The air coming in through the open windows was stifling as they drove. Traffic was heavy, and loud with honking horns. The noise of the North African city began to pound against Faith's head and she felt queasy again. Again, she debated asking him for water, but decided against showing vulnerability until she absolutely had to.

Once outside the city center, the traffic eased and their cabbie drove faster, Arabic music whining from his radio, beads swinging from his rearview mirror. He smelled of stale cigarette smoke and incense. Another wave of nausea swept over Faith, and for a moment she thought she was going to be sick. She eased her bound hands to her side so she could lean back against the seat and she closed her eyes as she rested her head back, concentrating on not throwing up.

"Were you lying about that man in the market, Lili?"

he whispered, this time in Spanish, presumably so the driver wouldn't understand.

"No," she said, eyes still closed.

"Why did he want to kill you?"

"I told you, I don't know." She paused. "Believe me, I wish I did."

"Why did you kill Escudero?'

"I don't know what you're talking about."

He was fishing—had to be. He'd read her note with the time and place of the weapons deal. He'd seen Escudero get shot, and he'd found her sniper hide, but he had not seen *her*. There was still no proof she'd been the one to fire on Escudero.

"You had the note—"

"It was for someone else," she said. "I had no idea what it was for—I just passed it on. The cantina owner asked me to do it. I only heard later about Escudero."

"And then you suddenly left the country?"

She said nothing.

"Were you sleeping with the cantina owner?"

Faith opened her eyes. He was looking at her in an unguarded way. He caught himself, and his features hardened again. But something she'd glimpsed in his face got to her. She remembered the way he'd felt in her arms, between her legs; the flowers he'd left on her pillow.

"It's none of your business who I was sleeping with," she said quietly.

"You slept with me."

Her face felt hot. "You used me," she said.

"And you were open to being used."

Her mouth tightened and she looked away, out the window, eyes burning. He was right, that's what cut. She'd been rendered vulnerable by her desire for the man who'd watched her nightly from the cantina shadows. And look where that had gotten her now. He hadn't even come to watch—he'd just wanted her information.

"Why did you want the note?" she said.

"I had business to finish."

"You wanted to scuttle the weapons deal?" *Or just kill the bodyguard?* But she couldn't say that out loud—it would prove she'd been on the knoll and had seen him.

He inhaled deeply, as if tempering frustration. "Like I said earlier, Liliana, *I* have the gun. *I* get to ask the questions."

The scenery changed as they drove, dense buildings giving way to sparsely scattered settlements, and in between, there was nothing but sand or dry flinty ground. Tension built inside her. She needed to get a better sense of this man before he took her too far.

"You left me flowers," she said, quietly. "You didn't have to do that—why did you?"

"You gave me a good night."

Faith clenched her jaw. A good night, in exchange for the information on the note—that's all it had been for him. For her…it had changed her life. She'd been on the pill. They'd used protection. But the stomach bug must have left her system vulnerable. And condoms were known to occasionally fail. Obviously hers was case in point.

"A very good night," he whispered after a few beats. "One of the best."

Faith's face grew hot and she clenched her teeth together as she continued to stare pointedly out the window. For the first time she was glad for the veil.

Omair's body went hard. He couldn't help it, sitting so close to her like this, talking about their shared night of pleasure, remembering how smooth and firm her naked body had felt under his, how she'd thrown her head back and cried out as she'd climaxed on top of him. He remained physically attracted to her in spite of the fact she'd just tried to kill him. Or perhaps even because of it. It just enhanced that air of danger she'd exuded right from the beginning.

But he didn't like the coincidence of her being both in Algiers and Tagua at the same time he was.

He wondered who she was working for—he'd get it out of her sooner or later. Clearly she wasn't of indigenous Maghreb blood. She was more likely freelance, a hired gun for MagMo, and a damn fine one. Omair understood mercenaries—he was one himself. And he could respect her skill. Yet he always worked to a code. He never took a job that went against his political philosophies, and he never harmed women or children. Which was why he was struggling with how to handle extracting information from this particular captive.

Not only was she female, he was attracted to her.

He reminded himself she could use his attraction as a weapon against him—he had to get over that. This was a woman who had no qualms about killing him.

And in aiming that rifle at him, she'd made herself an enemy to his family, to his country. And Omair wanted to know who'd paid her to do it.

Her head began to nod, her eyes flickering closed. Finally her head lolled onto his shoulder. She'd fallen asleep, her breathing calm and rhythmic, like it had been when she'd slept on his shoulder in Tagua. A strange rush of emotion filled Omair's chest.

Then he thought of Tariq in a coma, of Julie dead. Of his parents and Da'ud, murdered in their beds.

And Omair's heart steeled.

* * *

Faith woke in horror to find herself sleeping on her captor. She jerked back, self-hatred fisting inside her chest. This was the second time she'd fallen asleep on top of this man. What in hell was going on with her? She was a washed-up operative, that's what. And she didn't know what to do about it, or her baby.

Just focus on escape, survival. You can deal with the rest later.

Shadows were lengthening, the sun dipping low toward the western horizon as their taxi drew up alongside a cluster of flat, adobe buildings positioned around a dusty square where men stood around with whips in hand as they watched over small groups of camels. Beyond the camel market stretched an endless sea of desert.

Her captor held her close as he paid the driver.

Faith shot a look at the pods of camels in the square.

"What are we doing here?" she demanded.

"Buying transport."

"I'd prefer a Hummer," she said dryly. "Especially if we're going out into that." She jerked her head toward the sea of sand.

He laughed, and it irked her further. She yanked against his grip in a show of irritation, but he simply tightened his hold as he led her toward the camels.

"We can forgo this entire exercise right now, Lili, if you just tell me who paid you to kill me, and where I can find him."

"And what will you do then?"

"Kill him."

A fist of anxiety tightened in her chest. He had no idea the United States wanted him dead.

"And if I tell you who sent me, you're going to let

me walk free?" She laughed in his face. "I *know* what you people are capable of, I know your agenda. If I hadn't missed you in that courtyard I'd have done the world a favor."

His stopped dead in his tracks and a strange look crossed his features.

"What do you mean?" he said.

She flattened her mouth, glaring at him as she reminded herself to be careful in revealing nothing about herself, or STRIKE. Operatives were sent into countries that would not welcome knowledge of a foreign government soldier on their soil. STRIKE hits were usually surgical, in and out, and no U.S. fingerprint was to be left on any hit, which is why her unit, and country, would wash their hands of an operative if a job went sideways. Like hers was going now.

But her job was to kill this man. She could still salvage it.

"Fine," he said darkly. "We'll play this your way— the hard way."

He ushered her toward one of the camel pods being guarded by a leathery old Bedouin in dusty garb, and he began negotiating the purchase of two camels. The gap-toothed Bedouin then threw two saddles into the deal.

Faroud was clearly in his element out here as he laughed and chatted easily with the old desert man. But in spite of his apparent camaraderie, he had a definite command about his presence. His was the bearing of a man used to being in control, a man most likely used to money, and lots of it. Faith found herself wondering what their baby might look like. If it was a boy, would it look like him, or possibly like her own father?

Her mouth turned bitter at the thought of her father. Besides, what on earth was she thinking? She *couldn't* go through with having a baby—she couldn't be a mother. Tension wound tighter through her.

Her captor shucked his linen jacket and handed it to the old Bedouin. "Watch my wife for me while I saddle these animals up," he said with a nod of his head in her direction. "Then you can keep the jacket. We just married," he added. "She might get cold feet and try to run for the hills. If she does, stop her."

The old Bedouin cackled heartily, but took the request very seriously, edging toward Faith with camel whip in hand as Faroud expertly saddled the camels then went with the goatskins to the nearby well.

He returned, walking toward her, a goatskin full of fresh water in each hand, his muscles rippling under his damp cotton shirt. He'd rolled up his sleeves and he'd strapped her water pouch to his own hips. Condensation dampened the sides of his pants. Faith's throat tightened with thirst.

He grinned, and damned if it didn't make him look more devastating. But she knew what he was doing— he was showing her he was in control of the one thing she was going to need most in the desert. Water. It was going to be his interrogation tool. And his smile was to show her that he could be nice, as long as she cooperated.

He tied the water bags and rest of the gear to the saddlebags and then called the Bedouin to bring her to him.

She refused to go with the Bedouin, making her own stand, showing him she wasn't going to make things easy for him.

Irritation flared darkly across Faroud's features, and he stalked over to her, grasped her arm. Faith jerked against his grip, anxiety coursing through her veins at the prospect of leaving all civilization and heading into that sea of sand with him in control of her water.

"Don't think I won't hurt you in front of these men," Faroud growled through his smile as he hauled her over to the couched camels. "And don't think they'll care if I do."

He shoved her up to one of the animals. "Get on."

"I'm not going anywhere with you."

"I'm not asking."

Fear twisted through Faith now. She glanced at the sea of sand. The deeper they went into that searing desert, the more challenging it would be for her to find her way back, *if* she managed to escape. She had to make her move before they went too far.

"Get on," he repeated.

Faith tried to swing her leg up into the saddle but she was off balance with her hands bound behind her back and she stumbled as her pant leg twisted in the chador fabric.

He caught her, then lifted her chador and hoisted her up, his hands gripping her butt. And as she settled into her saddle, he brought his mouth close to her face, his hands lingering on her. "You still feel good, Lili."

Heat speared through Faith in spite of herself. "Go to hell."

"Been there, done that."

"Yeah," she said very quietly, "well, so have I."

It stalled him, and for a moment Faith couldn't read the look in eyes, but she felt a brief and strange moment of kinship. And as he took his hands off her she told herself she had to look for gaps like this in his psyche, and dig in. He wasn't the only one who knew how to play this game. If she was unable to escape, she'd best find his weak points before he found hers. And while he had water and physical control on his side, she had information.

He suddenly hit her camel hard on the rump. "Yaa!"

Faith almost fell from the saddle as the beast lurched to its feet.

"Would be easier to ride with my hands tied in front of me," she snapped, trying to regain her balance.

"I have no intention of making your life easier." He secured her camel to his own with a length of rope, and then mounted himself. Clucking his tongue, he flicked his new camel whip lightly against the beast's haunches. His mount rose and their little caravan ambled out of the market like wobbly ships into an endless sea of sand.

The sun was already low on the horizon, shadows growing long. Faith took note of her bearings—they were moving southwest.

Her first strategy would be to try to lull him into a false sense of complacency in the hopes he'd drop some defenses. Then she'd surprise him, take the gap, finish her job and find her way back to Algiers and to the safe house.

But as the shadows lengthened even more and her thirst grew more fierce, Faith wondered if she was going to have the physical strength. And another, deeper problem niggled at her—when the time came, would she actually be able to kill the father of her child?

Chapter 6

The sky was purple with dusk by the time they reached a dry wadi bed with a few straggling palms. The last dwellings Faith had seen were several miles back—there was nothing but desert and a night of darkness ahead.

Her captor halted their little convoy, dismounted, and couched her beast with a cluck of his tongue. The protesting animal folded its front legs, clumsily lowering itself to the ground.

"You can get off now," Faroud said.

Faith's legs were stiff as boards and she needed to use the bathroom. As she tried to maneuver her leg over the saddle, she once again got tangled in the wretched chador.

He took her arm and helped her off. But Faith's numb legs buckled under her and she cursed as he caught her in his arms, her chador hood coming off in the process. He held her gently and his eyes softened for a moment.

"Lili," he said quietly. "Don't make this so hard on yourself."

She shrugged him off, but stumbled again as she tried to get her feet to work. He caught her again, and he touched his fingertips to the cut on her forehead, where the concrete shard had sliced across her brow.

"I'll clean that up and put something on it."

"It's fine," she said, moving her head out from his touch.

He removed her sunglasses, veil and the chador. Faith felt relief in being able to breathe unfettered by fabric. Turning her around, he untied her hands. His movements were gentle and Faith cursed him for it. It would be easier to fight back—and kill him—if he was mean.

"How are your wrists?"

"Fine," she lied.

They'd already been chafed raw from the belt and he could see it.

"Look, I know what you're trying to do," she said. "But false sympathy is not going to work on me. I'm not going to suddenly bond with my captor." Immediately she regretted even uttering the words—already he was winning ground in a psychological chess game.

He chose not to reply. Instead he removed her watch from her wrist and as he pocketed it she swiveled and tried to make a run for it. But he lunged forward, grabbing her by a chafed wrist, and he had his dagger out before she could even blink.

He waved the blade of his jambiya in front of her face. The steel glinted in the dusk and she saw the hilt was embedded with jewels.

"I know you're an expert with a rifle, Lili." He touched the tip of the blade gently to her nose. "But I'm good with this. Very good."

Her eyes watered and dizziness swirled. She wasn't up to this. Already she felt dehydrated, sick, exhausted. She'd underestimated the rough toll the day—and pregnancy—had already taken on her body, and it rattled her composure.

He led her over to one of the palms and made her hug it as he retied her hands on the other side. Crouching down behind her, he began to unstrap the holsters on her legs, removing the pieces of her high-tech military rifle, including scopes and ammunition. It was his first opportunity to do this without any witnesses.

He then patted her down carefully, and very intimately, his hands moving up the insides of her thighs. Faith closed her eyes, gritting her teeth against the memories of the last time he'd touched her there.

She made a noise of protest when his hand reached too high between her legs.

"Sorry," he said quietly.

That shocked her. "You sound like you actually meant it," she said.

"I did." He carried the components of her rifle a short distance away and laid them on a piece of cloth. "I didn't choose to make you my enemy, Lili. You made that choice when you pointed your rifle at me. And you can stop being my enemy anytime you want by giving me the information I need."

"Right, and then you'd let me walk away alive, especially now that I've seen your face and can identify you."

He glanced up sharply. "What do you mean?"

"You know exactly what I mean."

"Why don't you explain it to me anyway?"

She shut her mouth, glancing away.

"I don't *want* to kill you, or hurt you." He examined

her nightscope as he spoke. "Thing is…" He began to screw the pieces of her rifle together. "I don't believe this is personal for you. I think you're a freelance contractor. And I understand—I've worked as a mercenary myself. But why die for a bit of cash? Why sacrifice yourself for the people trying to overthrow my country?"

Faith's pulse quickened.

"What country?"

He laughed dryly. "Don't try to play me for a fool."

Uncertainty wormed into her.

He wasn't acting like a man who'd managed to avoid being photographed—he'd seemed genuinely surprised when she'd mentioned being able to now identify him. And MagMo didn't have a country, unless he was referring to some abstract notion of unity. And she *really* didn't like the coincidence of him being in Tagua, and her now being assigned to kill him.

"Why were you in Colombia?" she asked.

"I told you, I had business."

"What would you have done if I hadn't fallen asleep in your arms that night?" she said. "How would you have gotten the note—because that's what you wanted, not me."

He glanced up sharply. "Oh I wanted you all right, Liliana, from the moment I saw you. But you were off-limits to me, until that note arrived and went right down your cleavage. *Then* your cleavage became my business."

"Would you have killed me for the information?"

"Someone finding your dead body in the morning would have alerted the cartel. I couldn't afford that."

"But otherwise you would have?"

His eyes hardened. "I will do whatever I need in

order to protect my brothers and my sister, their families, and my country. So my advice to you, Lili, or whatever your name is, is don't stand in my way, don't try and hurt my family, then I won't have to hurt you."

Confusion, uneasiness, snaked even deeper into her. This didn't sound like the Faroud bin Ali described in her dossier. And those cartel weapons in Colombia had been destined for MagMo buyers, so if he was a MagMo terrorist, why had he sat waiting in Tagua for a note so he could scuttle the deal?

"I don't understand why you'd want to intercept that weapons deal—"

"Shall we start with why you killed Escudero?"

"I told you. I just passed on the note."

"The longer you take to talk, the more difficult this is going to be," he snapped. "For both of us."

"Good, because I really hate the idea of suffering solo."

He scrutinized her, eyes narrowing, then he rapidly assembled the rest of her rifle.

She had to hand it to him—it was a prototype weapon, and while she could assemble it blindfolded, it had taken him mere seconds to do it, even in this dwindling light, even while talking to her. He clearly knew his stuff.

But he also had a vulnerable spot—his family. While this confused her, it gave her a window she could use into his personality. She recalled the look of profound grief on his face back on that knoll in Tagua and she wondered if he'd received news about his family back then. Whatever he'd heard on the phone, it had given him great emotional pain—this was a man who, while harsh, had deep capacity to care.

Perhaps that just made him more dangerous.

He slung her rifle across his chest and returned to his camel where he untied her sling bag and carried it back to his mat. Tension strapped over her chest.

Her pregnancy test was in there.

He couldn't find out about that. It was too private. It made *her* too vulnerable. He'd use it against her.

Panic licked through Faith as he upended the bag and the contents tumbled out onto his piece of cloth. He picked up her sat phone, and scrolled through the contacts and call log. Faith knew she was safe there— nothing was stored in her phone. He set the phone aside and turned his attention to her GPS, going through the menu.

"Are you American, Lili? British?" He spoke in English for the first time.

She didn't reply.

"Your GPS support language is in English," he said.

She still said nothing.

"Mine's in Arabic." He used the tip of his dagger to unscrew the battery casing on her GPS, then he removed the battery. He did the same with her phone. He examined her watch carefully before crushing and grinding it to a pulp between two rocks.

Conflict twisted through Faith as she watched him severing her last links to the outside world. STRIKE could have used any one of those devices to track her location. Now she was uncertain whether she even wanted to be tracked by them—at least until she'd ascertained exactly what had gone down with her disconnected evac number and that sniper up in the minaret. Again, she reminded herself there could well be a rational explanation for both. The evac number could be explained by a technical glitch. The shooter could have been part of the security detail for the meeting in the courtyard. It didn't necessarily mean she'd been set up.

He began to feel around the inside of her bag, looking for side pockets. Then he felt along the inside seam—too close to where she'd hidden the pregnancy test and photo of her mother.

"Faroud!" she called.

He glanced up sharply.

"Faroud bin Ali."

"*What* did you say?" He got to his feet, shock in his features.

"That's what you call yourself." She too spoke in English now. "Is it your real name?"

Slowly he came up to her, amazement on his face. "You don't know my real name?"

Her gaze flicked to the purse behind him. She had to get that wand and photo out of there.

"You tried to kill me," he said, "and you *don't even know who I am?*"

"I know you're a wanted terrorist with the Maghreb Moors organization. That's enough for me to pull the trigger."

"Maghreb? You think I'm *MagMo?*" He took another step toward her, and he stared at her for several long beats. A warm breeze rustled suddenly in the dry palm fronds above, like an ominous whisper of foreboding.

"I *know* you're MagMo," she said quietly, but doubt quivered through her. She'd been given no photo, and no biometrics indicators had been programmed into her weapon. Was it possible the CIA plant in the hotel courtyard could have made a mistake in identifying him as her target? No—that didn't make sense.

He laughed suddenly, loud. Hard. But stilled just as

quickly, and there was a dangerous new edginess in his body that was palpable.

"And that's enough evidence for you? Who are you? Who led you to believe I was MagMo?"

Uncertainty wormed deeper. She'd said too much.

"*Who* sent you, Lili?" he demanded, his voice going low, dangerous. "Who was following you back at the market—who wanted you dead?"

She remained silent and anger whipped through his body. He spun around, scooped up the GPS from the mat, held it in front of her nose.

"You have a route mapped out in here to a small settlement called Amar'at. Is that where you were going in such a hurry when I found you in the casbah? What's waiting for you at Amar'at, Lili?"

She turned her face away, heart racing.

"Let's try this again. You said you missed your shot when you looked down your scope and saw it was me. Who's '*me*'?"

"Santiago." Her voice came out thick. Emotion pricked hot behind her eyes.

"So you were sent to shoot an alleged MagMo terrorist and you were supposedly shocked to see that this alleged MagMo was actually Santiago from Colombia?"

Alleged.

Sweat prickled over her body.

"You really don't know who you came to kill, do you?" He spat the words at her, derisive, mocking.

And it cut.

"You expect me to believe that you lay up there on the roof, waiting for some man called Faroud bin Ali to walk into your crosshairs? How were you going to know it was Faroud, a sign? Please…don't tell me it was that Russian and his carnation."

Her face felt hot.

He threw back his head and laughed again. Then he leveled his gaze with hers, right up close, hard obsidian eyes boring into hers, and he very gently cupped her cheek.

"You're a good liar, Lili," he whispered softly. "Either that or someone is taking you for one wild ride."

Faith's mouth turned bone-dry.

"If you're *not* Faroud…then who are you?"

He looked at her in disgust, dropping his hand to his side. In silence he walked back to the blanket where he crouched down and picked up her purse. But he didn't feel around the inside again. Instead he tossed her GPS and phone back into the bag, along with the batteries and knife. A dizzying wave of relief washed through Faith as he resecured her purse to his camel bag. Her personal secret was safe.

For now.

Omair removed his sweat-drenched shirt and replaced it with one of the robes he'd bought at the market. He cinched the belt tight across his waist and thrust his jambiya scabbard into the front. Out of the corner of his eye he could feel his captive watching him from the tree.

He could have told her outright who he was, but he preferred to keep her unsettled. It gave him an advantage. And if she thought he was MagMo, and she felt this was reason enough to eliminate him, she surely couldn't be working for them. So who, then?

Who else wanted him dead?

Was it possible she'd been set up by someone to assassinate an Al Na'Jar prince without being made aware of what she was doing?

Nothing made sense.

It was imperative he find out who she was working for.

At the same time, Omair reminded himself she was a pro. She was capable of playing him. She could be doing so now with her talk of MagMo.

He wound the strip of cloth he'd bought at the market around his head, Tuareg style, leaving just a slit for his eyes—it was going to get cold tonight. He slung the rifle back over his chest and holstered his pistol beside his dagger. He then reached for a goatskin pouch, pulled out the stopper, and when he was certain she was watching, he took a deep, long swallow of water, his eyes holding hers.

She turned her face abruptly away.

Omair stoppered the water pouch and resecured it to his camel bag. Then he scooped up her chador and went over to her.

"Can you sit, please?'

"Excuse me?"

He placed his hand on his dagger hilt. "Please, just slide down the trunk and sit, a leg on either side of the tree."

Faith clenched her jaw and slid down, her legs parted by the tree. He dropped to his knees in front of her, undid her gaiters, then untied and removed her boots and socks.

She cursed. He was ensuring that if she did manage to bolt, she really wasn't going to get far. She would have done the same if the situation was reversed.

"Okay, you can stand up."

She pulled herself back up the rough palm bark and he untied her wrists, then rebound them, this time in front of her. He replaced the chador and veil, and then motioned for her to climb back on the camel.

Faith walked gingerly over sand still hot from the day's sun, small rocks cutting into tender, bare feet.

Once back in saddle, he tied her hands to the horn in front.

He'd effectively stripped her of shoes, water, food, communications and navigation equipment. And he'd inserted doubt into her mind for it to grow like a cancer. He was good. She had to be better.

Calm and steady, Faith. Stay strong. Wait for a gap.

But she knew she was weakening, and thirst was dogging her.

He swung up into his own saddle. "Yaa!" he called out as he kicked his mount into action. Hers lurched after it, pain searing across her raw wrists as she jerked against her restraints.

But hope flared hot and sudden in Faith as she saw he'd changed direction. They were now heading east— back toward civilization.

She didn't know why he'd switched direction, but she held on to that spark of hope, mentally fanning it to flame. Her captor had to stop to rest some time during the night. She'd make her move then. And she'd still be close enough to make it back to the city alive.

But as the hours ticked by the sky turned into a black blot filled with stars. A fat gibbous moon edged up over the horizon, painting the dunes silver, and Faith developed a terrible headache. Her throat felt raw. The muscles in her legs were cramping and she was becoming increasingly light-headed. She was also beginning to experience heart palpitations, which she knew was a sign of dehydration. In an effort to maintain blood flow to her vital organs, other blood vessels in her body were constricting.

With the clear night sky the desert temperature began to plummet fast. Faith started to shiver.

She knew that without water, confusion would soon set in. Finally would come coma, organ failure. Then ultimately, death.

If hypothermia didn't get her first.

She wondered at what point in this process her baby would start suffering.

The thought galvanized her.

"Hey!" she called out to him. "I need water!"

He responded by picking up the pace and jerking her in the saddle.

As the minutes dragged by, she began to loll in the saddle again and Faith realized she was losing sense of direction now. She jerked herself back into focus as they crested a dune and saw lights in the distance.

Her abductor brought their convoy to a standstill. He studied the distant lights with her nightscope.

Faith's heart kicked. It looked like a small settlement on the horizon. If she could just make it to those houses... She eyed the bag on Santiago's camel where he'd stashed her shoes, socks and other equipment. She'd need to take those first. And water.

He clucked his tongue, suddenly setting the camels in motion again, and to her surprise he aimed their caravan directly toward the settlement.

When they were about two hundred yards out from what appeared to be a few square, flat-roofed dwellings, he pulled her mount up alongside his, and leaning over, he untethered her camel from his.

He placed her camel's head rope into her fingers while leaving her wrists bound to the saddle horn.

"Go," he said quietly.

She stared at him. "What?"

"I said go."

"Where to?"

His lips curved and she saw the glint of teeth in the dark.

"That's Amar'at up ahead," he said with a nod of his head. "You're going to take me to meet your friends, Lili. Go to the location you had marked in your GPS. I'm presuming it's some kind of safe house. Ride to the house, call your contact to come outside. If there is more than one contact, call them all out. But tell them to keep at least five yards back from your camel."

"I don't know what you're talking about. There is no 'safe house.'"

He laughed darkly. Then his voice turned low, seductive. "Your denial is tiresome, Liliana."

He raised her high-tech night vision scope to his eye again. "The house you want is the third from the end of the row—that's the one for which you have GPS coordinates in your system. There's an old Toyota Corolla parked outside."

He lowered the scope and she heard a click as he took the safety off her rifle. "I'm right behind you. I'd advise you not to forget it."

He reached over and hit her camel on the rump.

Faith gasped as her camel lurched forward, and she struggled desperately to work the lead rope with her fingers while her hands were tied. Finally the wretched beast slowed a little.

Breathing hard and feeling warm again, Faith peered back over her shoulder into the darkness for signs of her captor following. But he'd vanished, like a shadow into the velvet desert night. Adrenaline spurted through her.

This was her chance.

If she could alert the occupants of the safe house to her predicament before he got to them, they might be able to help her fight him off, or at the very least alert her handler to the fact she was in trouble. At the same time, insecurity coiled low in her gut. Her handler, Travis Johnson, was the one who'd given her the dud evacuation number.

Still, she had little choice right now other than to try the safe house.

Slowly she guided her camel down the single dusty road that led between a few dun adobes. The settlement was eerily silent, flat white pumpkins gleaming ghostly in the moonlight atop corrugated tin roofs. She'd known Amar'at was tiny, but this…seemed off.

A breeze began to blow as the desert's thermal balance changed, sending the veil fluttering across her face, and caressing her bare toes.

Then she heard, before she saw, a flag, flapping softly in the breeze. This was it—Travis had mentioned a flag. He'd said it would be flying the colors of Algeria—green and white with red sickle moon and star, although she couldn't make that out in the darkness.

Using her fingers she managed to tug at the rope and halt her camel. Faith studied the house with the flag. It was in pitch-darkness. And as her vision adjusted, a chill sunk through her—the flag was tattered. Torn white drapes fluttered eerily from windows with no panes. The Corolla outside was rusted, broken windows, no tires. The driver's side door was missing.

"Hello!" She called out in Arabic. "Is there anyone here?"

A dog barked. A door banged in the neighboring house and a light came on in the window.

Faith nudged her camel closer to the front door of the dark flat-roofed dwelling. She thought she glimpsed Faroud's shadow ducking behind the wall at the back.

"Is there anyone home?" she called again.

Silence felt heavy. The desert wind whispered a soft omnipresent sigh around her and the ghostly torn drapes billowed.

A strange feeling of unease curled through Faith.

A neighbor came outside. He was holding a stick.

"What do you want?" he called in Arabic from his yard.

"I want to speak to the owner of this house."

The man eyed her warily as he came forward, his fist tightening around his stick. She could feel the anxiety in his posture, feel him wondering why a woman was traveling alone in the dark with no shoes.

"No one lives there anymore," he called, stopping a few yards away.

The unease sunk deeper.

"Are you sure?"

"Of course I'm sure. That house has been empty for more than a year, ever since the old man died."

More than a year?

This was not possible.

Faith's handler had informed her this was the house of a friendly contact who'd help get her out of the country in an emergency, provide her with papers.

"Maybe someone comes by every few days or so?" she offered.

The neighbor shook his head. "When the old man died his son left to find work in Algiers. He never returned."

A robed figure suddenly emerged from the front door

of the abandoned house. She squinted, unable to see who it was in the faded dark.

Then her heart fell.

It was Faroud—or whoever he was. Holding her rifle. He must have entered from the back, swept the house, and come out through the front. It's what she would have done to flush out anyone who might have been inside while keeping her covered at the same time.

He came slowly up to her camel, nodded at the neighbor who backed away at the sight of his gun. The man turned, scurried back to his house. The door slammed. Curtains shut, dimming the pale light that had spilled into the night.

Faith looked up. Stars—a whole milky band of them—arced across the sky. Amid the constellations she saw a bright falling comet. She concentrated on it, and wondered when it had all gone wrong.

And she wished at this moment she'd never met Santiago, Faroud, or whoever he was.

He took the camel rope from her fingers. She didn't resist.

"No one inside," he said quietly as he led her camel away, hooves crunching sand on the dark street. "It's been abandoned for a very long time. Whoever hired you, Lili—they didn't want you back alive."

Chapter 7

The band of stars moved across the black vault of North African sky as the moon grew small and high. The desert became a haunting ocean of undulating silver shadows and the vastness, the solitude, was formidable—no sound apart from the creak of leather, the chinking of camel rings and pots against the saddle, and the odd snort and huff from the animals. A bitter cold had descended with the clear air, and it was especially brutal after the day's heat.

Faith's toes and fingers grew numb, her thighs sore. She shivered uncontrollably. Her lips were cracking and her tongue felt uncomfortable in her mouth. On top of that her sense of disorientation was increasing and making her want to throw up.

He was winning, damn him.

The psychological coup de grâce had been the abandoned safe house. It had knocked her badly.

"So, what *did* happen to your safe house?" he called out from the darkness ahead. "Did your employers set you up to the kill the wrong man, then hang you out to dry?"

She gritted her teeth against the chattering. "I don't believe that was Amar'at," she yelled back at him. "It was some other village."

He stopped his camel and swung back.

"Oh come on, Lili," he said as he came alongside her mount. "You're a professional. You had to have had that GPS location and route burned into your brain."

"I got disoriented," she said, slurring her words slightly now—a sign of hypothermia setting in. "It could have been some other village."

But even as she tried to justify the missing safe house, doubt was stalking in the dark corners of her mind like a hungry jackal.

Her handler, Travis, had personally programmed the safe house route into her GPS. And because this job had been such a rush, he'd also personally prepared her equipment for the mission while she'd been in debriefing. Everything had been ready and waiting for her on the jet—the sat phone, long-range rifle, GPS, dossier. Travis had even marked the rooftop from which she had to shoot.

Faith had always trusted Travis with her life—she'd had to. He'd never set her up like this, would he? Not unless he'd been ordered to by someone higher up. The thought was like ice in her veins.

Was it possible STRIKE brass wanted to retire her? Had clearing her in debriefing simply been a ruse so they could set her up by sending her out here? But then why ask her to kill this man and tell her he was Faroud bin Ali?

"You know what I think, Lili?" His voice came out of the dark and it seemed to be in front of her, then behind, then to the side. She swayed slightly in her saddle, her mind reeling with another wave of nausea and confusion.

"I think the plan was for you to shoot me, then have you silenced with a bullet from the minaret, but the shooter from the minaret faltered because you missed, and for a moment he was unsure what to do. In that moment you escaped."

Faith shook herself, willing her captor to shut the hell up. Mistakes happened. There could be a rational explanation, and she'd find it. She kept repeating this to herself.

"What I need to know is why your people told you I was MagMo."

The jackals of doubt nipped closer.

"Can you tell me, Lili?"

"Could be mistaken intel." Her words came out thick, and badly slurred now. "Or you could be lying. The man in the minaret could have been your own security," she countered, her tongue feeling too big in her own mouth. "You could've put him up there to watch over your meeting."

"If he was my security detail I would not have killed him when he approached you in the market. And he would have shot you while you lay in waiting for me on the roof. Yet he only attempted to kill you after you'd fired on me, am I correct?"

A cold depression swamped her and she shuddered again with cold, almost sliding from the saddle this time. Her hands, bound to the saddle horn, stopped her from falling.

* * *

He was watching her intently, his black eyes glinting in the moonlight through the slit in his turban. The jewels in the jambiya hilt winked from his waist.

"What's your real name?" she said as her world began to spin violently, sickeningly around her.

"You first, Lili. What's *your* name?"

She flattened her mouth.

"You could have killed me in Tagua, Lili, while I lay naked in your bed. Why not then?"

"That was not my job in Tagua."

"Your job was Escudero."

She tightened her fingers on the camel horn, clenching her teeth. Her mind was growing weak, fuzzy, and his questions were coming at her like battering rams.

Suddenly he came at her with yet another tack. "What has Faroud bin Ali allegedly done to become a most wanted terrorist?"

"He…he's responsible for a recent jet bombing at JFK, and he's behind fresh injections of cash financing MagMo operations in North Africa."

Omair froze, reined in his camel.

"*What* did you say?"

"You heard me."

She'd just accused *him* of being responsible for placing a bomb on his own family's jet. And she'd claimed MagMo was the organization responsible for the bomb, yet MagMo had not yet made an official statement. Her intel was so bizarre he felt a sudden pang of pity for her. This highly skilled sniper had been hired for a bogus mission, and he was beginning to think she honestly believed she was killing a murderous terrorist.

His pity segued into compassion as he saw her almost slide from the saddle again. She was showing signs of fatigue, possibly even hypothermia and dehydration. A ripple of anxiety chased through Omair—he'd thought she would hold up better.

"We'll camp here for the rest of the night," he announced abruptly. Couching his camel, he dismounted, then took her camel by the lead rope, stopping it, as well.

From his saddlebags he removed a tarp and laid it out on the sand in the lee of a dune, then he untied her wrists from the saddle horn and helped her down to the ground.

In her weakened state she stumbled and fell heavily into his arms. And as Omair held her for a moment, a powerful urge to protect her rose unbidden through him. Urgency also nipped at him—he needed to get her hydrated and warm, fast.

Quickly, he helped her hobble over to the tarp where he put on her socks and boots, noting the slender arch of her feet as he did. Images of that hot night under her mosquito net in her room above the cantina assailed him. Omair shook himself.

Removing a heavy blanket from his saddlebag, he wrapped it around her shoulders then fetched the goatskin water pouch and lowered himself down onto the tarp beside her. He untied and removed her veil. Her complexion was wan in the silver moonlight, her eyes dark holes. He unstoppered the goatskin and helped her drink.

She swallowed hungrily, which gave him a sharp spark of relief, and Omair realized how much he hated having to pry information out of her. He did not hurt women—it went against his personal code. Especially this woman—he still felt something for her. And now that he was beginning to think she'd been deceived for some ulterior purpose, he was angered for her.

Omair built a fire and when the flames were crackling hot and orange and shooting small sparks up into the black sky, he seated himself beside her again.

"Any warmer?"

She nodded. He put his arm around her shoulders, drawing her close, and he rubbed her arms.

Finally he felt her stop shivering and he relaxed a little.

He put a pot of water on the fire to boil for tea and found a small bag of dates in his bags.

"That information you were given about me, Lili," he said, reseating himself beside her. "It's so wrong it would be laughable if it weren't so serious. Do you really wish to protect the identity of someone who has hung you out to dry like this?"

She stared at the flames, her face deathly pale.

"Lili?"

"My name's not Lili," she said, very quietly, a sad look filtering into her eyes.

Omair's pulse quickened. "What is it?"

"Faith."

"Faith?"

She glanced at him sharply, and her gaze held his for a long moment. Omair caught the gleam of tears in her eyes. His chest cramped, and he had to struggle against the urge to take her into his arms again, to hold, to comfort.

"It's an interesting choice of name for an assassin," he said.

"I didn't choose it, my mother did."

"Your father had no say?"

Her lips tightened and she glanced away. "I don't talk about my father," she said flatly. "Ever."

Omair inhaled deeply and offered her the bag of dates. She reached for it without hesitation, taking a handful and beginning to eat.

"Faith who?" he said calmly, quietly.

"Just Faith," she said.

"It's a start," he said, putting the packet of dates in his pocket. He believed her—that Faith was her name. He'd seen the way her eyes had shot to his when he'd spoken it. And her father was a sore point. He filed this information away.

"I suspect we have a common enemy in MagMo, Faith. The man I'm hunting is the organization's new leader. I believe it is he who is ordering the deaths in my family."

She looked slowly up into his eyes. "You mean the man they call *The Moor?*"

"The New Moor," Omair said. "Not the old man who was recently captured by the U.S. military after an attempted biological attack on the States."

Faith swallowed, her gaze holding his, intense. She was silent for several beats and wind sighed up along the ridge of dunes behind them.

"I heard about the attempted mass suicide attack and the FBI agent who helped stop it," she said finally. "But I didn't know MagMo had a new leader."

"I just learned this news myself while in North Africa posing as a weapons dealer seeking to replace the stock lost by MagMo in Tagua."

"So you *were* posing as someone friendly to Mag-Mo?"

"That is correct."

"So…someone *might* conceivably confuse you with being a terrorist."

"A terrorist called Faroud bin Ali?" He snorted softly. "You're trying to rationalize what's happening to you, Faith. Face it, we're on the same side, united against MagMo."

She rubbed her face in frustration. Omair took the boiling water from the flames and threw another log on the fire. As the fire crackled he made sweet tea and handed her a mug.

"Careful," he said. "The enamel is hot."

She wrapped the edge of the blanket around the steaming mug and cradled it between her hands, drawing warmth from it. Omair was relieved to see color returning to her cheeks.

He made a mug of tea for himself, then reseated himself on the blanket beside her. He liked the feel of her next to him, and he sensed the start of a fundamental shift in her. He told himself to play it carefully from here.

She sat staring into the flames, sipping her tea, clearly mulling over what he'd just told her.

Turning to him suddenly, she said, "That man with the white suit and red carnation—"

"The Russian?"

"I didn't know he claimed he was Russian."

"He's been dealing arms for decades. His specialty is Chinese guns to Africa and Cold War munitions to the Balkans."

In the firelight he could see the carotid at her neck pulsing fast. Omair was hit with another memory flash of bodies tangling, skin slick with sweat, a fan turning slowly above them, sounds of the jungle outside. His own pulse quickened.

"How did this Russian get you to meet with him in the hotel courtyard?" she asked.

"I was going to supply him with guns. He was buying for MagMo, to replace the cache that blew up in Colombia."

"Jesus," she said softly, glancing away for several beats.

"Who did you think he was, Faith?"

She said nothing.

"Faith, if your people asked that Russian to set me up, they had to know he was an arms dealer, and that MagMo numbered among his top clients."

She drew the blanket tighter around her and stared into the fire. Wood popped and crackled. Omair poked at the embers and sparks spattered up into the thick blackness.

Silence descended around them.

"I love this world, you know?" he said, nodding out toward the endless shadows of dunes under moonlight. "There's nothing quite like the desert at night, the profound silence, the timelessness of the sand, the history. It's like this in my country."

"Are you going to tell me which country?"

Omair sat silent for several beats. "Faith," he said quietly, touching her arm. "Tell me who hired you—it will help me find the Moor, I am certain of it. You are my one link after all these weeks in Africa."

Faith looked deep into his ink-black eyes. He'd taken his turban off and his hair gleamed in the moonlight. The flames made his skin glow copper. He looked like a desert warrior—both frightening and devastatingly handsome. His looks had done it for her back in Colombia. They did it for her now, too. Again, that little whispering thought crept into her—would her baby look like its father? Would the child want to know who its father was one day?

No. She couldn't go through with it. Could she?

Her mouth turned dry.

Even if she wanted to, it was a ludicrous idea. Yet looking into this man's eyes now, she felt a bond, just knowing his baby was inside her. And the urge rose in her to share. With him. Anyone. Again, she fought it down. She was exhausted. She couldn't think about these things now. What her captor was telling her was fundamentally devastating, if it was true.

"I'm sorry," she whispered. "But I can't tell you who sent me."

"They're not worth protecting, Faith."

"I...have a contractual obligation," she said. She was still a soldier, and a good soldier's duty was not to question, or even to know the context of every military decision. And the revelation of STRIKE—a government-sanctioned hit unit—would undermine the United States. It would start wars. She couldn't be responsible for that—and she still couldn't be certain this man was telling the truth.

"I can't trust you, either," she said. "I don't know who you are, or why I was given the wrong information about you, and there's always the chance you're just messing with my head."

"Fine," he said, sipping his tea. "I can understand this. As I said, I've worked as a soldier for hire and have had similar contractual obligations myself. A mercenary has a reputation to uphold—it's a small world."

"Can you say who you've worked for in the past?" Faith said.

He pursed his lips, studying her intently, as if weighing how much to reveal to her. "For the most part," he said slowly, "I worked for the FDS, but I'm on my own now."

Surprise stabbed through her.

"The *Force Du Sable?* The private military services company based on São Diogo?"

"Yes."

Faith stared at him, her mind reeling. "The United States has used the FDS before, in sensitive situations, particularly in Africa."

His eyes narrowed sharply. "This is important to you—the partnership of FDS with the United States?"

"And smaller nations use them, too," she added quickly, cursing herself for her slip. "Those without strong armies to defend themselves under attack."

His gaze bore into her and Faith felt her cheeks warm under his intense scrutiny. The memory of him in the cantina sifted into her mind, him walking toward her over the old wooden floor, his shirt open to his waist, his skin gleaming, the fit of his jeans crying out for sin.

The look in his coal-black eyes that fateful night had held similar dark intent to now. But while she'd thought the intent that night was purely carnal, she now knew better. He'd wanted something from her all right, and it wasn't just sex. She swallowed, embarrassed by her foolishness.

Was she being as foolish and blinded by him now? Because if he really had contracted to the FDS, technically it made them allies.

And it made it even more absurd to think STRIKE had ordered her to hit an FDS operative. Ex-operative, Faith reminded himself. People—times—change. He could have done a job since leaving the FDS that had made him a U.S. target now.

She moistened her lips. "And now you're working

solo, hunting this New Moor, because you believe he's attacking you and your family?"

"And you can help me."

"It's very important to you, family."

"It's everything."

He said it with such finality it was like an underscore.

"Do you have a wife, children?"

The question seemed to take him aback, then he laughed lightly. "I wouldn't be sleeping around with women like you, Faith, if I was married."

Like a blow, his words rammed into her gut. She told herself she was being ridiculous. She'd gone in wanting a hot one-night stand. So why was she hurt? Why did she feel his words diminished her in some way? She looked away.

He noticed.

"Faith?"

She met his gaze, and a moment of realization hung between them.

"What I meant, Faith, is that I take the vow of marriage very, very seriously and there is no room for it in my life, nor for children of my own. There can't be. Mine is a warrior's duty now."

She wondered what he would say if he knew she was carrying his child, and Faith snorted. "A warrior's duty?"

He shrugged.

"It sounds so...ancient."

"It is."

She thought of the antique-looking jambiya he carried—the kind passed down by tribal leaders for centuries, and she wondered where he'd gotten it.

Faith finished her tea, and before she could even

think to ask more questions of her own, an overwhelming wave of nausea and fatigue hit her. She set her mug down on the tarp, and put her hand to her brow as her world began to spin again.

"Are you all right?" He touched her arm with such care, it made her chest hurt. She shook him off.

I'm pregnant and it's playing havoc with my body and my brain, never mind this mission.

"I need sleep," she said.

"Sleep then," he said gently. "I'll keep watch."

"I thought I was your captive, not that you had to protect me from capture." She spat the words at him out of frustration.

He grinned and Faith's heart did a funny torque at the sight of it. She hadn't seen him smile, really smile, not even in Colombia. The role he'd played there had been dark and sullen.

"Remember, we're on the same side, Faith. You can help me find the Moor."

"It would help if you told me your name," she said as she lay down, curling onto her side under the blanket, using the robe he'd put there for a pillow.

He nodded. "Yes. When you can tell me who you work for, I'll tell you my name."

She lay there, looking up at his profile etched against the firelight, the moonlit dunes rising behind him. And as she began to fall asleep, he said suddenly, "Who ordered the hit on Escudero—was it the same person who wants me dead?"

She jolted back, and cursed inwardly. He was still playing her, allowing her to drop off and then hammering her with an abrupt question.

"I didn't kill him," she replied wearily.

He put his head back, his neck tense. "Look, there's

no use for this charade, Faith. I know you did it. I saw your sniper hide, and I have forensic evidence that will no doubt prove it was you."

Anxiety punched through Faith, and she edged herself onto her elbow quickly.

"What evidence?" she said as she fought back another wave of nausea and dizziness.

"I found some strands of hair and a very unique shell casing at the sniper hide. I've sent the hair for DNA analysis, and the casing to an arms expert with a private forensics firm."

"What?" Her heart hammered.

"I have a private investigator doing the work for me, and lab is one we use often—"

"We? Who's *we?*"

He ignored her question. "They worked up a DNA profile from the hair. It was originally blond, but dyed dark." He paused. "Just like Liliana's."

Her mouth went dry. She'd seen him pick up the casing, but she hadn't known about the hair.

"There was also a partial print left on the shell casing. My investigator started running the DNA profile and print partial through various international databases four weeks ago. I believe, Faith, if I send him some of your DNA and your prints, we *will* find our match."

Something akin to terror washed through her body.

If her DNA profile and prints had been run through *any* law enforcement or other major government databases in the U.S., even covertly, an alarm would have instantly sounded in STRIKE computers. And if it looked as if someone was investigating her in connection with a hit on foreign soil, it would be enough to scrub her from the program.

Proof of a U.S.-sanctioned assassination on Colom-

bian soil would be devastating to her, to STRIKE, to the
U.S. government, and they'd do everything to bury her.

"You have no idea what you just did," she said, her
voice going hoarse. "You signed my death warrant."

His eyes flashed. "How so?"

"When did you say your investigator started running
my profile through databases?"

"Four weeks ago."

During her debriefing.

Faith's heart sank like a cold, hard stone. Perhaps
she'd never been cleared. Perhaps, because of this man
and his private investigator, alarms had triggered a need
to retire her. That could be why she was assigned such
a rush hit, and why a sniper might have been lying in
wait to kill her.

She dropped her face into her hands, feeling sickeningly overwhelmed suddenly.

He put his arm over her shoulders again, and Faith
leaned into him—she couldn't help it. His solidity, his
warmth, his humanity, was a comfort in the darkness
she felt inside. Ironically, the man she'd been sent to
kill, the man she believed to be the enemy, might just
be her last ally in this world.

If he was telling the truth.

"Why," she said softly, "does it even matter to you
who killed Escudero? Why did you need to run my profile through databases?"

He was silent for a long while.

"Maybe, Faith, I just couldn't excise you from my
mind. Maybe I wanted to know who Liliana really was."
He glanced down at her. "Maybe Lili bewitched me
so that I was driven to do it in spite of my priorities."

Surprise fluttered through her.

"And then, when you showed up in Algiers, I had

to wonder if the same person hired you to kill both me and Escudero—and why."

He leaned forward as he spoke, and ever so softly caressed her cheek. In spite of herself, a primal need for comfort, for love, to be held, unfurled inside her and she had to fight the desire to just lean into his touch, to give into him entirely.

"The Escudero hit had nothing to do with you," she said quietly, a fog of cool depression, a blanket of exhaustion swamping her mind as she started to fade again. She couldn't fight all this anymore, not without rest. The pregnancy was taking a serious toll on her body on top of it all.

"Sleep now," he whispered gently. "We have a long, hot ride ahead in the morning."

Beyond exhaustion, Faith did fall asleep, curled on the tarp under the blanket by the fire.

Omair watched her, listening to her breathing, unsure of what he was feeling right now. The fire popped and camels munched on dry tufts of vegetation nearby, the sound of them comforting in the desert night. He needed to go hobble them, he thought, so they wouldn't stray in the darkness.

He looked down at Faith again.

"I don't know who you really are," he whispered. "But you're one hell of a woman, and I intend to find out."

She murmured in her sleep, and Omair felt a strange pang in his heart. God help him, he was falling, absurdly, for a woman sent to kill him, and it had started the moment he'd first laid eyes on her in that cantina on the banks of the Tagua River. And she *could* still be pulling the wool over his eyes.

Omair fed more wood onto the fire, mulling things over. Then he slung her rifle across his chest, went out to secure the camels, and climbed to the ridge of the dune behind them. Using his satellite phone he called his private investigator in the States, all the while keeping an eye on Faith asleep by the fire.

"Run the DNA profile and print partial from Tagua again, this time couple it with the first name Faith, and see if anything comes up."

Reception was bad for some reason, and the P.I. on the other end asked Omair to repeat himself. He did, louder. And he glanced down at Faith wondering if she'd heard, but she lay still, apparently fast asleep.

"The name could be an alias, but I feel there's a very good chance it's real," he told the investigator. "I suspect she's American, and if she's a private contractor the odds are she came from military or law enforcement background before she hired herself out. If so, her DNA profile could be in older military databases, or in law enforcement databases."

Omair signed off and saw that he'd missed a call. It was from Zakir. Quickly he dialed his brother in Al Na'Jar, fearing bad news about Tariq.

Zakir answered on the first ring and cut to the chase. "He's out of the coma."

Relief burned fierce into Omair's eyes as he clutched the phone. He looked up to the sky for a moment, and said silent thanks as he choked up.

"What is the prognosis now?" His voice was thick. There was a beat of silence, and Omair's chest tightened in trepidation.

"Tariq believes he failed Julie. As a doctor he felt he should've been able to do something to save her on the runway, before the next explosion."

"That would have been impossible."

"Try telling that to him. He's beating himself up over it—it's like he's lost the will to live, Omair. Our brother is badly scarred, in more ways than one. It's going to be a long and difficult road ahead for him."

Omair heard the pain in his blind brother's voice, and he hurt, too, for Tariq. For Zakir. "How're Dalilah and Nikki holding up?"

"They're being strong for him. If anyone can work magic on Tariq, it'll be Dalilah. He always loved her most. She's the one who could make him smile."

Affection filled Omair's chest. Dalilah could make any man smile.

"I should be there," he said.

"No, it's best you continue with your mission. Get the man who is behind this."

Hearing Zakir's voice steeled Omair's will—his mission was to stop the threat against them all, and he was going to do just that, no matter how long, or where, it took him.

"And the media has bought the line about Tariq's passing?" he said.

"It's been in the news for the past four weeks."

Sometimes, thought Omair, the biggest lies were the easiest to believe.

"It's the right thing," he said. "It will keep him safe, it'll help him heal."

It would also put Omair in immediate line of fire as next in line to the throne. He glanced at Faith. Who was he kidding—he was already in the crosshairs. And Faith was his answer to whoever was behind this, he was certain of it.

Omair trudged down the dune and made straight for his camel. Untying Faith's bag, he returned to their small camp and once again emptied the contents onto a mat a short distance away from her. The fire crackled softly as he felt around the inside lining of the bag. He'd seen the way she'd kept glancing at the bag, and he'd begun to suspect she might be trying to divert his attention from something hidden in there.

His fingers touched something that felt like a stiff piece of paper under the lining. Omair frowned. He turned the bag inside out and discovered an opening along one of the side seams. He dug his fingers into it, removing a crumpled, faded and torn photograph.

The snapshot was of a woman, maybe in her late twenties, holding a baby in what appeared to be a christening gown. The woman was seated, and judging by the style of her clothes and hair, Omair figured it had to have been taken twenty to thirty years ago. A male hand rested on the woman's slender shoulder. There was a wedding band on his ring finger and from his sleeve it looked as though he was wearing a military dress jacket. The rest of him had been ripped out of the photo.

Omair frowned, then shot a glance at Faith. The moonlight threw pale silver on her hair, and firelight played soft shadows of gold and yellow over her skin. Why, he wondered, had she brought this photo with her on a hit? Could the baby in the photo be Faith? Could this woman be her mother? There was some resemblance, and if the photo had been taken about thirty years ago, the timing was about right for this to be Faith and her mother.

I didn't choose it, my mother did.... I don't talk about my father. Ever.

Omair wondered if Faith had torn her own father out of this family snapshot, out of her life even, and the notion sent a strange pang to his gut. The fact she had this damaged memento with her on a mission told him her mother was important to her, and that her past had been painful. Faith's words sifted into his mind.

Family is very important to you...

He held the photograph nearer the flames, examining it more closely for telling details, trying to make out what kind of military jacket the man was wearing, what country.

Faith rolled carefully onto her side where she lay by the fire and edged herself up slightly, trying to see what he was looking at now. She'd woken to hear snatches of his conversation on the ridge. While she'd feigned continued sleep she'd heard him telling someone to run her DNA profile and print again, this time using the name Faith. If she wasn't already doomed, she would be once her name went into the databases.

A jolt of electricity shot through her body as she realized what he was looking at.

Her photo.

Faith dug her fingers into the tarp, inching up a little more. Laid out on the cloth beside him, along with her veil and the belt he'd used to bind her wrists, were her GPS, sat phone, batteries, knife and scope.

He set the photo down with her other belongings and began carefully feeling around the seam of her bag again. She could not allow him to find the test. The last thing Faith needed was for her captor to find out she was pregnant. *Especially* if he began to suspect the baby was his.

Fear swelled in her. She had to get away from him. Now. While his guard was down, while he thought he was winning her over.

And once she escaped, she had to find proof that

STRIKE might have set her up. Those were her priorities.

She'd flee as far and fast from her captor as she could, then she'd break strict security protocol and call Travis on his personal cell number. Years ago she'd hacked into the system and found the number. She'd been digging for information on Travis—her life, after all, was being placed in his hands, and Faith thought she might need a backup plan one day.

Well, that day was here.

And when she did call Travis, she was going to test him. Because either her captor was lying, or Travis— her own people—was lying and truly did want her dead. And if the unit did want to retire her there was no going back. STRIKE would attempt to finish the job no matter where in the world she tried to go. The only answer would be to find a way to completely disappear and start anew.

Faith slid her fingers toward a stone lying at the edge of the tarp. Levering herself up, she tossed the rock into the darkness to the right of her captor. It landed with a soft thud on sand.

Her captor stiffened and glanced to his left. Slowly he reached for the rifle at his side.

Faith curled her fingers around another bigger rock, and hurled it after the first, farther into the darkness. It made a dull thud. The camel nearby snorted.

Her captor got up and began to move into the darkness, toward the noise, weapon ready. Faith surged to her feet and crept rapidly toward the blanket with her things. She grabbed the knife and belt, and like a cat she stalked up behind him in the sand, any sound she might have made being drowned by the now complaining camel in the dark.

She found her captor trying to placate the animal. From behind, Faith lunged, looping the belt over his head. She yanked it tight.

He gasped for breath, but before he could reach behind him, she pressed the tip of her blade into his back.

Chapter 8

The prepaid cell phone inside the top drawer of Isaiah Gold's desk rang. His pulse quickened as he yanked open the drawer and answered it.

He listened carefully to what the caller had to say, then killed the call. Isaiah leaned slowly back in his leather chair, mulling over what the envoy of the New Moor had just told him—the Russian arms dealer had been killed in Algiers by Sheik Omair Al Arif, who himself had escaped the bullet of the STRIKE operative sent to assassinate him.

And because Faith Sinclair had missed, the MagMo sniper positioned in the minaret had in turn hesitated and failed to take *her* out. The MagMo sniper had since been found stabbed to death in a market in the casbah.

Both Sinclair and Al Arif had meanwhile gone to ground. Whether together or solo was still in question.

Isaiah reached for his pen and tapped it rhythmically on his desk blotter. What really troubled him was not so much the fact Sinclair had failed to assassinate Omair Al Arif—that could still be done, and the Moor saw the attempt as being a good faith move on the part of the senator. No, what concerned Isaiah was the fact Sinclair must have by now realized she'd been set up by her own country. She could wreak untold damage if she took this to the media. The revelation she was an assassin sanctioned by the United States to kill on foreign soil could take down the U.S. government, kill Sam's bid for the presidency. Which would in turn scuttle Isaiah's own ambition to be a quiet and driving force behind one of the most powerful offices in the world.

Sinclair was a dangerous loose cannon. She had to be found and eliminated, stat.

Isaiah rubbed his brow. Sam didn't need to know about this. Not yet. It would distract him from the campaign. He'd handle it himself.

He scooped up the prepaid cell, pocketed it, and left his office to take a walk into the park. Once he was near the fountain he dialed an unlisted number and listened to the phone ring.

Travis Johnson answered.

As Faith tightened the belt around her abductor's neck, she kept her blade pressed into his lower back. And she realized, from the bottom of her soul, she was unable to kill the father of her baby. Especially now that he'd created doubt about his identity, and her own unit.

Adrenaline screamed through her blood as she torqued the belt tighter, strangling his breath.

"Drop the weapon," she whispered, hating the fact her body was trembling.

The rifle fell with a soft thud to the sand at his feet.

The camel moved on, still hobbled.

She tightened the belt more, and he reached to grasp her wrist. But she pushed the tip of the blade into his skin.

"Don't move."

He stilled, but was rasping for breath.

She had to be careful not strangle him to death, just render him unconscious. But he held on, fighting it. Then slowly she felt his body give, and he slumped to the ground. Faith rolled him quickly onto his side, into a prone position, and checked his pulse. Relief rushed through her—he was still alive. But relief was followed by a sharp disgust at her own actions. Something had changed profoundly in her. She couldn't do this kind of work anymore. But now it was not about work, it was about survival. Hers and the tiny life growing inside her.

With shock Faith realized just how raw and protective a maternal instinct could be, and how much that instinct was driving her right now.

Perspiration broke out over her lip as she quickly bound his hands behind his back, using the belt. Then she bent his legs back, as if he was kneeling on his side, and strapped his wrists to his ankles.

Breathing hard, Faith scooped up the rifle and raced back to the blanket. She slipped the photo of her mother into the side pocket of her cargo pants then felt along the lining of the bag. Sweat was drenching her body— he could come around any minute now.

The pregnancy wand was still there—it had slid around the inside of the lining to the base of the purse where it hadn't been immediately evident to him. Faith reached deep inside the lining, tearing fabric as she yanked it out.

In the quavering firelight, the blue line was still

there. She stared at it. It looked so surreal, under this desert sky, a lifetime away from life as she knew it, the father of her child lying unconscious nearby. Suddenly overwhelmed, Faith lowered herself slowly and sat on the blanket for a moment, trying to gather herself.

Another clutch of emotion chocked her throat as she recalled him making love to her, how vital and alive she'd felt.

We're on the same side.... You can help me....

Remorse filled her, but she slid the wand into the side pocket of her pants with the photo. Gathering up her GPS, Faith reinserted the battery and powered it up to get her bearings. She then reconnected her sat phone battery and attempted dialing the evac number one last time. It rang three times and once again clicked into the same out-of-order voice mail message. Her captor's words echoed through her mind.

They set you up to kill the wrong man...take the fall... hang you out to dry...

Faith turned slowly around to look at him, and an eerie sensation crawled over her skin. It was if he was speaking to her.

She had to get out of here before he woke and started messing with her head again. Because he had undeniable power over her, both mentally and physically. And she was weak in the face of it.

The fact she was carrying his child didn't help—it was eating at her, burning her up inside.

Family is everything.... There is no room in my life for children of my own.

Faith inhaled deeply. Her only real family had been the army, and then her unit. Now even that might be questionable. If so, she was totally on her own. She had to be strong.

Faith pulled the robe she'd been using as a pillow over her head, and bound a piece of cloth around her head like a turban.

Slinging her rifle over her chest, she tucked her knife into her hiking boot and went over to where he lay. Cautiously she slid his satellite phone and pistol out from the holsters at his hip, then she reached around his waist for his dagger. He was lying on top of the scabbard and she had to heft him aside to access it. His body felt solid, strong. A memory of him naked slammed so suddenly and sharply through her head that Faith dropped him in shock. Her heart thumped in her chest.

She glanced at his face. In the moonlight his powerful features looked like a sculpture, and again she heard his voice in her head....

Why sacrifice yourself for the people trying to overthrow my country?

Faith's hands began to shake. But she steeled herself, reached around his waist again. This time she managed to grasp the hilt of his jambiya and remove both it and the scabbard from his belt. Slowly, Faith unsheathed the blade.

The steel glinted in the lunar light and the weapon felt good in her hand. The bone from which the hilt had been crafted was still warm from his body, and it was clearly antique. It had been inlaid with tiny brass stars and ruby-red stones that glittered with life in the firelight. Momentarily mesmerized, Faith stared at the dagger, and she couldn't help wondering who had possessed it over the passage of time, what warriors had once ridden over these sands with this jambiya thrust into their scabbards? In this region of the world a jambiya was a status symbol, almost mystical to some.

Wind soughed suddenly around Faith, lifting the

ends of her robe, making sand rustle and scurry like a living thing at her feet.

Mine is a warrior's duty. That's my lot. It's a lonely one, but an honorable one....

Her attention shifted back to his face, his aristocratic features, his thick dark lashes, the power that once moved through his limbs now momentarily gone.

Who are you—this father of my baby?

A sheik fighting some ancient war? A terrorist defending an ideology? A mercenary for hire? Someone else entirely?

Would she ever find out if she fled now?

Faith closed her eyes. This man was the closest she'd come to a relationship, as absurd as that might seem to some. But the man she'd fallen for had been Santiago. And now?

Now she didn't know.

Had they met in another time, another life, she wondered if it might have been different. And Faith couldn't help herself—she knelt down beside him and then, as if touching a tiger sleeping in a cage, felt carefully for his pulse again. It was there. Soft, then a little harder. Emotion swelled sharp and sudden into her eyes and spilled down her face. This was ridiculous, she thought, angrily swiping her tears away.

He *could* be exactly who she'd been told—Faroud bin Ali—and he could've been psychologically manipulating her all along.

Don't think about it...just get out of here, find out if Travis set you up...then take it from there...

Fresh resolve burst through her body. Faith gathered up her bag, the blanket, and ran to where she'd last heard the camels.

She found them, ghostly shapes in the moonlight.

She dropped to her knees in front of one, fumbled to unhobble its foreleg.

Copying her captor's method, she took hold of the lead rope and, clucking her tongue, tapped the animal's haunches with the camel whip. Protesting, the camel reluctantly folded its legs and knelt on the sand.

But as Faith was about to climb into the saddle, she hesitated again, remembering the blooms he'd left on her pillow, the way he'd made love to her, how he'd watched her all those nights in that miserable cantina, the tenderness she'd felt in his strong arms as he'd helped her drink her tea. Her chest hurt.

She *wanted* him to be innocent, dammit. And she couldn't just leave him out here like this. He'd die without transport, water.

There were two water skins on this camel, one of them almost a third empty. Faith dismounted, and, fingers working fast, she untied the partially empty bag and placed it next to the fire. Then she dragged him over to the tarp. He was heavy, and her compassion was costing her energy and hydration. She covered him with another blanket she found in the saddlebags and then brought the remaining hobbled camel closer to him.

Hesitating, she touched his hair. *Goodbye, Santiago,* she whispered. *It's been one hell of a ride.*

And, mounting her camel, she galloped fast into the night, aiming in an easterly direction. As she rode, Faith felt a weird ache in her heart. She was going to miss him, as crazy as that might seem, and it made her realize how pathetically alone she'd become in her life. She told herself she wasn't worthy of more. She was an army brat who'd moved from base to base, never even trying to make friends. She hadn't wanted anyone coming to her house to see her mother's bruises, to witness her father's drunken bouts. So she'd kept to herself, no peers.

Then she'd run away and ended up being bounced from one foster home to another. At the first possible opportunity Faith had joined the only family she'd ever really known—the military. There she was treated as an equal—her skills earned her respect. She always had backup.

That was her family, and her loyalty continued to lie with her country. She *had* to believe she could go back there, that Travis would offer a reasonable explanation.

But as she rode on, Faith was unable to quash the increasing bites of doubt, the obvious gaps in logic, or the anxiety over her pregnancy and what it would mean for her future as an assassin, or a refugee from her own country.

Nine hours later the sun was white-hot and high. Heat shimmered in oscillating waves off the sand and shadows were nonexistent. Faith was hunched forward in her saddle, listing with the rocking movements of her camel. Even behind her sunglasses she had to squint to avoid the blinding glare. When she thought she saw a clump of palms on the distant horizon, Faith prayed it wasn't a mirage.

As she neared, relief welled through her—it was a wadi fringed with straggling trees and the possibility of shade once the sun had passed its noon zenith. Faith raised her long-range scope to her eye and scanned the horizon. About a mile beyond the wadi, in a slight valley to the east, she could see a few dwellings.

It was time to break protocol and call Travis. Faith also felt she'd put in enough distance between herself and her abductor to rest a while under the trees until the desert cooled a little.

The wadi was dry as bone dust. Faith hobbled her camel and crouched beneath the straggling fronds of a palm. It offered no respite from the heat. She took a small sip of water and powered up her captor's sat phone. It was her first opportunity to look through it.

Unlike hers, his contained a list of contacts. The support language was Arabic. He'd entered no name for himself. She scrolled quickly through his contact list.

It included names like Julie Belard, Hunter McBride, Jacques Sauvage.

The rest were mostly Arabic and some entries were first names only, like Rafiq, Zakir, Dalilah, Tariq, Nahla. Faith frowned.

The name Jacques Sauvage felt familiar somehow. Where had she heard that name before?

She could dial one of these numbers—it might be a way to find out who her abductor really was. In case her child would one day want to know who its father was.

Anxiety rushed through Faith at this thought. She hadn't yet decided what to do about the baby, so why was the notion of becoming a mother settling like this in her head?

Taking a deep breath, she used her own phone to dial Travis Johnson's unlisted number.

She listened to his phone ringing half a world away in Washington, D.C. Calling the private numbers of STRIKE personnel had potential to jeopardize safety of the members, or compromise the entire unit. Doing this would cost Faith down the road, but if her captor was right, the move might save her life.

"Hello?" Travis said as he picked up. He sounded like he'd been sleeping.

"It's Faith."

There was a long beat of silence. "Where are you?" His voice was suddenly crisp. "Your tracers haven't been operational."

So he *had* tried to track her.

"The mission was accomplished," she lied.

Two seconds of silence ticked by.

"What is your present location?" he said. "We'll send an evac—"

"Why didn't the evac number you gave me work?"

"We'll go through it all in debrief. Just tell me where you are now."

So he knew the evac number was inoperational—he didn't question or deny it.

"I'm at the safe house."

Dead silence filled the space between them. Her heart thudded loud in her ears. She'd called his bluff.

He cleared his throat. "Okay," he said slowly. "Give me the coordinates of the house." But while he spoke slowly, it sounded as though he was suddenly moving somewhere rapidly, possibly to his office, to a computer, somewhere he could track her GPS, or this sat call. Urgency bit into Faith. She had to get off her phone and dismantle her GPS battery. *Fast.*

"You have the coordinates of the safe house, Travis." She said coolly. "You're the one who programmed them into my system."

"You can't be there—"

"Why, because it doesn't exist? Because Faroud bin Ali doesn't exist? Because the operative in the Algiers hotel courtyard was actually a Russian arms dealer who's now dead?"

Silence.

Faith's heart dropped like a cold stone.

"I get the message, Travis," she said quietly.

"Faith, we need to go through this in debrief. Just give—"

"It's been nice knowing you."

"Faith—wait!"

She killed the call, a cold, white anger slicing through her. Faith rapidly dismantled the phone battery then scrabbled in her bag for her GPS. She'd powered it up back at the camp at least nine hours ago—they could have been tracking her all that time. She hoped to God there wasn't already a chopper in the air.

Faith scrolled rapidly through her GPS mapping software, memorizing the details of her location, the route she wanted to take. If she made an abrupt turn northwest from this point it would lead her toward the Atlas Mountains. From there she might be able to cross into Morocco unnoticed. It was her only option. She knew someone there who could potentially help her create a false ID and disappear.

With shaking hands she removed the GPS battery and tossed it under the tree with her sat phone in disgust.

Nausea and exhaustion rolled over Faith. She yanked the turban off her head and rested her head back against the rough bark of the palm for a moment, trying to gather her wits. And then the reality sunk in—hard.

There was no going back now, no going home.

No more Faith Sinclair. She was done. Retired.

Good as dead to the world.

Faith began to laugh, a little maniacally, at the thought. She was *free*. Solo.

She stilled, a chill washing through her now. She was wrong. It wasn't just her. She had a life growing inside her.

Faith closed her eyes. Heat was like a blanket. Trying to calm her breathing, she placed her hand on her tummy. And as she sat like this she was overcome by a sense of presence. She wasn't alone. She had a tiny little life with her. And a sweet warmth filled her chest.

Maybe there's a reason you came to me, she whispered, holding her tummy as a mounting hot breeze started to swish through the dry tattered leaves overhead.

Maybe I need you in my life now.

An overriding primal maternal urge swelled through her, filling her chest with a sensation Faith couldn't even begin to articulate. She had a child inside her. It didn't matter who the father was, it was *her* baby.

And for the first time since the stick had turned blue Faith just sat and tried to absorb, process, the reality; the depth and breadth of what this was going to mean to her. A baby. She was going to be a mom.

The corners of her lips curved as hot tears pricked behind her eyelids.

She wasn't without fear. Faith didn't know the first thing about being a mother. But she could try. She certainly couldn't go home and be a soldier any longer. She had no family anymore, not one soul in this world she could truly turn to, or lean on.

She *had* to do something different. A new name. A new country. A child.

It would be a good, solid cover.

And as the idea took hold and grew powerful inside her, it steeled her will to survive. She was going to stay alive for this baby. She was going to get out of this mess, secure a new identity, and she was going to raise her child, protect it.

A sense of newfound purpose began to hum in every

molecule of her body. This baby, thought Faith, had just become the most important driver in her life.

And it was good she didn't know the true identity of the father. That way she'd never be tempted to break cover by trying to find him. And if he never knew he had a child, he wouldn't ever come looking. This way Faith could sever every possible link with her past, which was imperative, because if she left the slightest chink, there would forever remain a chance STRIKE could find her.

She was going to give this baby a future.

And no one in this world was going to take that from her.

An hour later the hot breeze had turned into a steady wind that felt like a hair dryer turned to full blast. Faith bent into the wind as it flapped her robes, dried her skin, cracked her lips. Sand was beginning to lift in spindrifts off the ridges of dunes, getting into her eyes, her nose, gritting between her teeth.

But she was determined to keep going as long as she could before hunkering down against what appeared to be a mounting sandstorm. She needed as much distance as possible between herself and the last known GPS location STRIKE might have on her. If there was any consolation, the coming sandstorm would obscure her tracks.

The wind started to make a whistling noise, and the sky began to darken with clouds of sand. For a moment Faith thought she heard a chopper thudding above the noise, above the haze, but it disappeared. Or was perhaps a trick of her mind.

Omair examined the tracks around the wadi, furnacelike wind whipping at his robes as he held on to his camel rope. Faith appeared to have rested here awhile, but now her trail veered suddenly off to the northwest, away from civilization—and potentially water. He frowned, wondering why. Then he caught sight of her discarded GPS battery and sat phone lying in the sand, and he pursed his lips, thinking.

If she'd powered up her GPS and used her phone to call the people who'd hired her, and discovered she really had been set up, she might've feared they'd come after her. Which would be good enough reason to dismantle any tracking device and head off in an opposite direction.

He mounted his camel, and followed her new path, into the teeth of a hard wind that had the makings of an imminent Sahara sandstorm. He moved fast, because the blowing sand was beginning to obscure her tracks.

He figured she didn't have too much of a lead on him. From the passage of the stars in the night sky Omair figured he had been unconscious maybe an hour, max. He'd used a shard of flint dug from the sand to slowly saw through the belt that bound him. It hadn't taken that long.

His advantage now was speed and proficiency on his camel, and knowledge of the terrain.

At the same time he knew he'd never have made it this far, this fast, without the water she'd left him, or the camel. It told Omair she cared. She trusted his story enough not to have killed him, but not enough to stay with him. He couldn't blame her—she had no idea who he really was, and she'd likely set out to try to verify things on her own.

But the Sahara was a dangerous place, and Faith wasn't going to get far without knowing where to find more water.

And Omair wanted to find her, alive, not only because she was the one link he had to whomever was trying to assassinate him, but because, deep down, he wanted to get to know this woman better.

He'd never met anyone like her. He almost smiled at the thought—she'd make one hell of a partner if he ever considered having a relationship that meant more than staying the night.

About an hour later, moving at a good clip, he crested a ridge and saw her. She was bent into the wind, traversing a valley of flinty ground beneath a wall of rocky caves, heading toward softer sand in the distance. She'd changed from her chador into the robe she'd been sleeping on, a turban wound around her head. *Smart woman,* he thought. It would be easier to travel alone looking like a man. And from her northwest course she was heading straight toward the hostile Atlas Mountains. He figured she might be aiming for Morocco.

Omair kicked his camel into a gallop, an odd rush of excitement swirling through him as he barreled down the dune after her.

Travis Johnson listened carefully to Isaiah Gold's words. He wasn't concerned about the call being traced—the prepaid cell phone Gold had instructed him to buy guaranteed anonymity.

"It's imperative she be found, stopped," Gold said. "Before she brings everything down."

Travis moistened his lips. This was an opportunity for him, if he played his cards right. Already Gold had intimated there'd be a position for him in the new regime if the senator won the election, and all indications were that he would.

"Does the senator know about this?" Travis said into the phone.

"This is my show," said Gold. "It has nothing to do with the senator. But if we do get into the White House, I will need men like you on my team."

Travis inhaled slowly, a soft excitement trilling through him.

"She called a few minutes ago," Travis said.

"Did you trace the call?" He could hear the bite of adrenaline in Gold's voice.

"I got a read on both her sat phone and GPS. Her last known coordinates place her a few miles out from a small desert settlement called Maktar. When she called, I saw from the system that she'd powered up her GPS nine hours prior to phoning in. The route she'd taken to that point puts her on a trajectory toward Maktar, but I suspect she'll have changed direction after making contact."

"We'll need to use an Algerian team from this point," Gold said quickly.

"You mean MagMo operatives?"

"We can't sanction U.S. personnel—this has to stay under the radar. I have a contact. I'll get back to you as soon as I have further instructions." Gold killed the call.

Unease tightened in Travis's chest.

Collaboration with known terrorists was a risky career move. But he was now in this to the hilt—he stood to lose as much as anyone else if his operative wasn't silenced, and soon.

But he also knew Faith.

She would not make this easy for them.

Chapter 9

The wind shrieked along the unprotected ridges, mounting in speed and strength as clouds of sand began to blot light from the sky. Faith bent into the wind, trying to keep in the leeward valleys to avoid the brunt of the rising storm. She saw the black shape closing in on her too late.

It was him!

Adrenaline exploded through Faith and she kicked her camel into a high-speed gallop. But he was the better rider and was gaining on her fast. In an effort to shake him, Faith veered suddenly to her left, trying to head up the dune, but the move cost her. The sand was soft, deep and the dune steep. Her camel faltered as he cut rapidly up her inside tack. Lurching off his mount, he smashed into her, knocking her from the saddle.

Faith slammed to the ground, air whooshing out of her lungs, sunglasses flying off her face. He landed with force on top of her, crushing her into the sand, the rifle slung across her back ramming into her spine. He grabbed her arm, twisting it painfully behind her.

"Don't move," he growled near her ear. "Or I will break it."

She lay dead still, trying not to breathe in a mouthful of sand, terrified the blow to her stomach had hurt the baby, or that the rifle still strapped to her back would go off.

When she didn't move, he rolled off and turned her onto her side to face him. Wind whipped the loose ends of his turban and his eyes, unprotected by shades, showed not anger, but deep concern.

Conflicting emotions warred inside Faith—relief that he was alive, that she hadn't inadvertently killed him. But she also hated him for tracking her down. She'd been on the verge of freedom, a new future. So close in her mind that she'd been able to taste it. And as she felt the pregnancy test in her pocket pressing against her thigh, she grew terrified he'd find out.

She *had* to escape from him before that happened. But before she could try to wriggle out from his grasp, he leaned forward, cupped her face, and pressed his lips down hard on hers. Faith's breath caught in her throat.

She resisted, trying to push him off, but as he forced her lips open under his, a deep, raw need swelled sudden and fierce in her, overriding logic, her desire to flee. Her eyes burned with emotion, and grabbing him around the neck she kissed him back, desperate for something she couldn't define, desperate to block out the world, the death, the killing, the hate. His tongue found hers, tangled, and kissing her deeper, he gathered her closer in his arms. Tears spilled down her cheeks as she ached to dig even deeper, faster, harder for something she knew she'd never reach. At the same time a need swelled in her to share with him the secret of her child. Their child. But she couldn't. She didn't even want to know who he really was anymore. She had to get away from him.

She pulled back suddenly, heart hammering, breathless.

His eyes were dark burning oil, his features etched with raw desire. He was her Santiago again, and Faith hurt in her heart for something she couldn't have.

"You didn't kill me," he said softly.

Faith reached for his dagger, sheathed at her waist. "You shouldn't have come after me."

"You left me water. You left me a camel. You didn't have to do that."

She yanked the dagger out of the sheath, rolled onto her side and kicked up to her feet. Taking a step back, she waved the blade in front of her. "If you come one step closer I'm going to be forced to finish the job."

He got slowly to his feet, eyes fixed on the dagger—his dagger.

"What do you really want, Faith?"

"I want you to turn around and get the hell away from me, just leave me alone." She had to yell now, over the scream of mounting wind higher up on the ridge.

In a predatory crouch, hands out at his sides, he came toward her. "Give me my jambiya, Faith. I can help you." He came closer.

Panic sparked through her and her mouth went dry. "I don't know who you are," she yelled. "Or why they want you dead, but you're not my business anymore, so please, just turn around and walk away and nobody gets hurt!"

The wind gusted, tearing at his turban. He came even closer.

Faith felt cornered, confused, conflicted. Adrenaline pounded into her blood.

"My name is Omair," he called out.

Something stilled inside her. She didn't want to know this. It was easier to cut him—everything—out of her life if she'd never have a way to find him again, or even a clue to start looking. She'd decided at the wadi. It was her focus now, the drive go somewhere safe, anonymous, to have her child in peace, where she could learn to be a good mother.

"I don't need your help." Her voice came out wrong, and she knew he'd sensed her flailing.

"You know that your employers hung you out to dry, don't you, Faith? That's why you dismantled your GPS back at the wadi. That's why you threw away your sat phone, and came northeast, isn't it? You think they're coming for you. You're on the run for the Moroccan border."

She wavered, unable to move for an instant, like a rodent trapped by a snake's mesmerizing—and deadly—stare.

"I can get you out of Algeria," he called out. "Without you having to cross the Atlas Mountains. Those peaks—they'll kill you, Faith. You need to know where to find water. There are bandits out there. And if you don't get out of the open in the next few minutes this sandstorm is going to kill you first." He lunged suddenly for the jambiya.

But she was fast, whipping around, and coming back at him in a tackle she rammed her shoulder into his gut with all her might. He was flung sideways, the momentum of her attack sending him tumbling down the steep dune. He stretched out his arm, trying to halt his fall, but gravity sent her crashing down on top of him. They rolled to the base of the dune, coming to rest in a hot, breathless heap.

He didn't move.

Faith pushed herself off him and her heart stalled when she saw his face—it was bloodless, his features twisted in pain.

"Oh, God," she whispered, touching his face. "What happened?"

He groaned and tried to move onto his side, but gasped. His hand went to his shoulder. "I think it's dislocated," he said.

She'd probably done it by landing on his shoulder as he tried to halt his tumble down the dune with an outstretched arm, and she'd hit him in a vulnerable position, aided by gravity and momentum.

Faith placed her hand on his shoulder. Through his robe she could feel the head of his humerus bone bulging below his shoulder joint. It was an anterior dislocation and she knew this kind of injury was excruciatingly painful.

Her whole body began to shake with an overload of adrenaline. The sand was a stinging fog around them, and up higher in the dunes the wind began to screech like a tortured banshee.

"We've got to get some cover—" she yelled. "I need to help you reduce the dislocation before the muscles spasm!" Faith bent down, trying to help him to his feet by his good arm. He gasped in pain as he staggered to his feet. Around them the sound of the storm grew louder, the sky darker.

But just as she hooked his good arm over her shoulders taking the brunt of his weight with her back, a deep throbbing sounded over the wind, and the black silhouette of a chopper emerged over the ridge.

"Get down!" he yelled, dropping back to the sand and pulling her down with him. He covered her with his good arm as the helo thudded above the cloud of sand. It came back for a second pass, lower this time.

"It's looking for me," she yelled. "They must've got a reading from my GPS."

"Fools," he growled against her ear. "If they come any lower the sand will get into the engines and bring them down—" A stream of bullets suddenly riddled into the dune, passing just inches away from them.

Faith pushed to her knees, pulse racing as another barrage of bullets cut across the dune below them, spitting up a line of sand.

He grabbed her sleeve, yanking her. "Get down!"

But she jerked free and began to stumble up the soft dune toward the ridge, reaching for the rifle still on her back.

"You can't shoot! Sand could jam it!"

Unslinging her rifle, Faith dropped to her knees halfway up the dune, just as the dark shape of the helo emerged again above the swirling sand.

Whipping the stock to shoulder, Faith squinted into the scope. Sand stung her face, and the wind tore at her robes, but she remained steady, her body going quiet, and focused as her finger curled gently around the trigger.

Omair stared in awe at the sheer beauty of this woman shutting herself down in the middle of a sandstorm, quieting her pulse in the height of pressure. The thudding grew deafening again. The helo came closer, closer, probably reading their presence with heat sensors. She fired. Then again.

The chopper banked sharply, rising above the swirling sand, and the thudding grew distant. Omair thought he heard engines sputter, then there was no sound other than the scream of the wind.

She knelt there on the dune above him, arms hanging limp at her side, rifle still clutched in her hand. And as the adrenaline ebbed, the excruciating pain returned to his shoulder. They had to find shelter. He scrambled to his feet and holding his bad arm against his torso, he staggered up the dune toward her.

"Come!" He grasped her by the arm. "You're going to die out here," he yelled. "If we move fast we can get to the caves in the valley before the brunt of the storm hits!"

She slung the rifle back over her torso and stumbled down the soft sand dune behind him.

"Not much farther," he yelled as they reached the rockier, flintier ground of the valley.

They ducked, panting, into the first cave, a large cavernous space where the air was hot and still. Outside the storm grew to a deafening roar, and swirling sand completely blackened the sky.

Omair sunk down onto a rock, coughing as he held on to his injured arm. She touched his shoulder gently. "You need to let me reduce that dislocation, right now."

He glanced up. In the dim light her eyes were luminous, unguarded and filled with worry.

"God, you're beautiful," he whispered.

Faith's chest clutched at the rawness, the honesty, in his voice, his features.

"It's the pain talking," she said crisply as she unwound his turban. "Can you stand? I need to get your robe off so I can see what's going on."

He struggled to his feet and she undid his belt then

carefully helped him lift his robe over his head. He sucked air in sharply as his bad arm moved.

"I'm sorry," she said. "This is my fault. I must have hit you at a bad angle."

He grinned through his obvious pain. "You mean you weren't *trying* to hurt me?"

A wry smile toyed with her own lips. "Sit," she said.

"You saved my life out there, Faith," he said as he acquiesced. "Firing on that helicopter was a dangerous move. If that rifle had been choked with sand it could have blown up in your face."

"We both would have died if I'd done nothing," she said. "They could see we were there—they had to have been using heat sensors. We didn't stand a chance."

"Who are they?"

"I don't know."

He angled his head.

"I honestly don't know. Now sit still."

His torso was as buff and dusky-skinned as she remembered and Faith couldn't stop a fleeting memory of lying naked in his arms. She swallowed, focusing on his shoulder, but she could feel her cheeks warm.

It was definitely an anterior dislocation, with the bulge of the humerus in front. This was the most common kind of shoulder dislocation and it was fairly simple to manipulate manually into place—if done quickly.

Faith knelt down in front of him, conscious of his eyes hungrily taking in her every move, of his proximity, of the way he was holding his body stiff with pain.

"Try to relax," she said, taking his injured arm and bending it gently at the elbow.

Carefully, she rotated his arm and shoulder inward toward his chest, making an L-shape.

She took a deep breath, then laughed lightly at her

own nerves. "I haven't done this in a while. The last time was when…" She caught herself and fell silent.

"When?"

"On a job…" She began to slowly but steadily rotate the bottom of his injured arm outward, keeping the upper arm still. "Can you make a fist?"

He did. Holding on to his fist, she pushed slowly. He groaned deeply, but she continued, working against the pain and protesting muscles, carefully pushing and twisting, coaxing the bone to work back into the joint, and suddenly there was a soft popping sensation as it slid into place.

Relief washed out of him in an exhalation of breath. His eyes were watering.

She released a huge breath of her own, one she hadn't realized she'd been holding.

"We need to strap up your arm, immobilize it for a while."

"We?"

Faith met his eyes, and something shimmered in the hot, still cave air between them. She became acutely aware of her pregnancy, of the fact she could see desire in his eyes. Of the fact that she wanted him in spite of herself, and her situation.

"It's a figure of speech," she said quietly as she began to unwind her own turban. Her hair fell loose to her shoulders.

"This turban cloth will have to suffice as a bandage. Maybe if the camels haven't wandered off—"

"They won't, not in this weather. They'll be hunkering down together."

"Good. Then we can use a strip of blanket and some rope from the saddlebags to fashion a better sling when we find them later."

He was silent, holding his good arm out as she bound the injured one to his torso.

Her fingers lingered, just a little too long, against his skin. It was just as she remembered—smooth and warm and supple over iron-hard muscle. Another flash of memory sliced through Faith: their bodies tangling, slick with sweat, under her mosquito net as the fan turned lazily above them and monkeys screeched in the jungle outside.

"What is it, Faith?" he asked, his voice thick. The intensity in his eyes had grown so dark it was almost unnerving.

She swallowed, her face growing hotter. "Nothing." She tucked the loose end of the cloth into the makeshift bandage. "There, that should hold."

But before she could move away, he reached out and touched her hair. Gently. Then he stroked his fingers down the side of her face.

Goose bumps rippled over her skin.

Omair thought she looked like an angel right now. A healing angel. Her hair was like a spun gold halo in the strange orange light filtering in from the storm. Her skin glowed from the heat. It reminded him of the heat in Colombia, of how she'd haunted his dreams ever since.

In spite of his best effort Omair had not been able to excise her from his mind. It was true that he'd sent her hair for DNA analysis partly for selfish reasons— he'd been curious. And maybe a part of him wanted to find her again, for reasons he'd not been quite ready to articulate to himself.

But now he could.

Now he wanted to get to know Faith much, much better. Trouble was, those selfish reasons were now braided inextricably into his mission because she still held secrets he wanted. The information Faith retained could change his life, alter the course of his country.

"I like your hair blond, natural," he said quietly. "And while I loved the sensual, rich brown of Liliana's eyes, I like your amber eyes more. They're more open, more honest this way. Softer, more kind. Gentle."

She glanced away sharply, pulse hammering at her neck. "Don't do this," she whispered. "I know you just want information."

"Faith—"

She shook her head, held out her palm and got to her feet. She went to stand near the entrance to the cave, and she stared out at the storm.

"What did you mean, Faith, when you said I'd signed your death warrant by searching for your identity?"

She inhaled deeply and was silent for several beats, clearly struggling with how much to tell him.

Finally she spoke. "If the people who hired me think someone is investigating me for a hit they assigned, they will do everything and anything to eliminate me, to keep themselves safe, anonymous."

"And how exactly will they find out I am investigating you?"

"They're powerful. They have contacts."

He frowned. This sounded bigger to him than a simple contractor. This sounded like it might even be the work of the new and exceedingly powerful Moor.

But if MagMo did actually hire her, why lie and tell her that *he* was MagMo? Because she might not accept the job otherwise?

"Faith, there's no doubt in my mind now that you were framed to kill the wrong man, and die in the process."

"I know." She looked at him, clear and direct, a tone of resignation in her voice. "And the reason I was sent out here to be framed and killed is probably because you started searching for me." She snorted softly. "Got to love the irony there." She dragged her hands over her hair. "I should never have slept with you in Tagua."

"I'm glad you did."

She stilled, met his gaze.

"I suppose," she said softly, her voice coming out husky, "that if I hadn't taken you upstairs to my room you might have killed me for the note anyway." She paused. "Maybe you should have. Then I wouldn't be in this predicament now."

He got to his feet and came to her side. With his good hand he cupped her face, tilting her chin up. "I'm pleased you're in this predicament—for very selfish reasons, Faith."

"Yeah, so you can find the Moor and all that, I know."

"No," he said darkly, lowering his mouth to hers.

Panic flared suddenly in her eyes, and she stepped back, glowering, her chest rising and falling.

"Faith, I can help you," he said. "I can get you out of Algeria without you having to cross those Atlas Mountains alone."

"I don't want your help. The only reason you're offering is because you think I still have information to offer you. I *don't*."

"You really don't trust easy, do you?"

She laughed dryly.

"Tell me something, Faith," he said, taking a step closer to her again. "Who is in the photo you carry with you. Your mother?"

Something flickered in her eyes, a flash of vulnerability perhaps. And then her features shuttered, and Omair felt he'd just lost her.

"Did *you* tear your father out of the snapshot?"

"You don't know it was my father—you're fishing."

"But it was, wasn't it?"

Silence.

"My guess is that he was in the military, perhaps still is. I could see from the sleeve of the dress jacket he was wearing."

Anger tightened her face and energy seemed to roll off her in waves.

"What did he do to you, Faith?"

"So you found a photo and now you think you can play shrink. Go to hell, it's none of your business." She walked to the other side of the cave entrance. She stood there, shoulders tight, arms folded over her stomach as she watched the storm outside.

Omair came up to her, touched her shoulder gently. She tensed, but this time she did not back away.

"Faith—"

"I'm sick and tired of the head games, you know that? I've told you all I have to tell."

"Faith, look at me, please." He turned her to face him and he saw the emotion pooling in her eyes. His heart clenched. He touched her cheek softly with the palm of his hand and tears spilled suddenly down her cheeks.

"Damn you," she said. "I don't want to talk about my family, my past, and you keep hammering me and telling me that you're doing whatever it is you're doing because *you* have this blood honor and you love your family, and you love children, but you—"

He silenced her with a kiss.

She stiffened for a moment, then softened under him. Omair felt a rush of warmth go through his body as she opened her mouth hungrily to him. He could feel the dampness of her tears, taste the salt of them on her lips, feel the desperation in her body. Kissing her, he edged her back into the cave.

Her hand moved up his torso, touching his bandage. Then she stilled suddenly, stepping back. Her eyes were luminous, her lips plumped with his kiss, her nose pink and her breathing was fast and light.

She stared at him for several long beats, something strange entering her eyes—a hollowness, a yearning, an edginess. It simmered into the air between them.

"I was an army brat," she said quietly. "I was born on a base, christened on a base, and we moved from base to base for my entire childhood. It wasn't easy to make friends." She paused, rubbed her face. "You're right, my father was military. He was a decorated war hero. But he also suffered from PTSD, for which he never sought help. Instead he turned to alcohol and he abused my mother." Her jaw hardened. "And she let him do it. She *let* him hurt me, too."

The sudden aggression in her voice was laced with pain and frustration and it tore at Omair's heart.

"And then my mother just gave up and died. She took a handful of pills on my twelfth birthday, of all days, right after she'd given me my first ever bouquet of flowers. White roses." Her voice went thick. "Those white flowers you left on my pillow..." She shook her head as she struggled to tamp emotion down. "They just took me right back. You have no idea."

"Faith—" He reached for her, but she held up her hand.

"I need to tell you now. I need to get it out. I blame my father for my mother's death. He killed her, and she allowed it to happen. He stole any hope I'd ever had of a childhood, and she allowed that to happen, too. I *hate* them both for it. I…I vowed never to be weak like my mother, to never let a man get the better of me. I ran away after she died." Faith shrugged. And Omair sensed she'd been trying to shrug this off her entire life. But it was a part of her—it had shaped her into the woman she'd become.

"Long story short, when I was eighteen I joined the U.S. Army where I found a family of sorts, people who respected me for my skill. I excelled as a sniper. I was better than the men." She smiled wryly. "Then I went private."

His body tensed—he'd been right. She'd been with the American military.

"Why private?" he said.

"I…I wanted to travel." And Omair knew instantly she was lying now. He could hear it in her voice, read it in her eyes. This last bit didn't fit, but he let it go, for now, because the rest was brutally honest and he could see her struggling to tell it.

"I never took a job I didn't believe in, Omair," she added. Then she swallowed. "I believed my Algiers assignment was right, too."

His gut tightened at her use of his real name. It made this thing blossoming between them feel real and it sent a heady rush through his body.

"I honestly thought you were Faroud bin Ali." She moistened her lips. "And when you put doubt in my mind, I could no longer follow through, even when I had the chance."

He knew this was true, or he'd be dead right now. He reached out, drew her toward him, and she didn't resist. Instead she leaned into him. Heat pooled low in his belly.

"I'm so sorry, Faith," he whispered into her hair, inhaling her scent. "To hear this about your past, your family, is painful when I have something so rich with mine. I cannot imagine not having that bond."

She closed her eyes as his hand moved down her back.

"My name is Faith Sinclair," she murmured quietly against his torso. "I can't see much harm in telling you that now."

Omair stilled inside, his pulse quickening.

"My father was Colonel Russ Sinclair. He died two years ago from alcohol poisoning. My mother's name was Melissa. You can check it out."

She pulled her robe up over her head and began unbuttoning her shirt, her eyes dark and mysterious, her lids heavy.

Omair's heart began to thud.

She slid her shirt off her shoulders, reached behind her back and undid her sports bra. She let it drop to the cave floor as her breasts swelled free, rose-colored nipples tight with lust. She seated herself on a rock, and unlaced her boots, then she took her off her pants. She stood, naked, in front of him, the sandstorm screaming outside. Inside the cave the air felt hotter, thicker. She came toward him, her breasts rounded, her nipples pointing at him.

Omair felt his head spin as all his blood headed south.

She crouched down in front of him, unlaced his boots.

"Sit," she said.

He did, and she removed his boots. She reached for his pants zipper, undid it and slid her hands inside, moaning softly with pleasure as she found him hard and ready. She helped him remove his pants, and without preamble, she straddled him, lowering herself ever so slowly down onto his erection, her eyes holding his.

A groan began to build low inside his chest as he felt her sliding onto him like a tight, hot, glove.

She pressed her breasts against his naked torso and began to move her hips.

He clamped his good hand on her butt. "Wait," he managed to say. "You haven't asked me for my last name, now that you've told me yours."

But she pressed her mouth against his, rocking her hips rhythmically against his. "I don't want to know," she murmured against his lips. "I don't want you to give me any reason to change my mind."

Chapter 10

A quiver of unease shot through Omair at her words, but it was shut out by the sensation of her smooth, firm inner thighs rubbing against his skin, the feeling of her buttocks working against his groin, her body going slick with perspiration.

Visions of their night in Tagua swirled through his mind as he yanked her naked body closer with his good arm. He took one of her nipples in his mouth, his tongue flicking, teeth scoring.

She groaned in pleasure, her hands going around the back of his head, her fingers sinking into his hair as she arched against him.

Faith wanted to exist only in the moment, to think about nothing else but this—no past, no future. She fisted her hands in his hair, opening her legs wider as she sank deeper onto him, her vision spiraling as she rocked against him. His range of movement was limited because of his arm, and her lust was fueled by a sense of control.

She needed control. And she didn't want to know who this man was, or where he came from. Because as soon as the storm cleared, she was going to take a camel and head straight for Morocco. Once she crossed that border she was going to disappear into the fabric of Africa.

It was an easy continent to hide in, compared to others. She could work her way south, toward Angola, Botswana, maybe Namibia or South Africa, as far as she could possibly get from STRIKE's last location on her.

And the sense of promise that came with the idea was exhilarating. She threw back her head and bucked harder against him, her movements turning aggressive, her skin going slick against his, and a scream began to build inside her chest as the storm raged outside.

He grabbed the back of her head, bringing her mouth back down to his, his tongue entering, tangling with hers. Every nerve in her body began to tingle, and her vision turned scarlet.

He murmured in Arabic against her mouth, but though she couldn't catch the words, the seductive sound made her move more urgently, the friction driving her wilder. His hand clamped suddenly to her hip, stopping her.

Faith stilled, and looked into his eyes. His features were etched with aggressive lust, his eyes black and dangerous. Perspiration gleamed on his muscular torso.

"Don't...move," he whispered.

A slow smile curved her lips and she thrust her hips into him.

He dug his fingers into her buttocks, attempting to restrict her movement. "Don't..."

Omair was breathing hard, inside her to the hilt and she had all the control, and he wasn't ready to come, not until he'd made sure she had. Call him too alpha. Call him power hungry, domineering...call it yet another battle of wills.

She tried to thrust against him again, a wicked smile curving her lips, her eyelids swollen with lust. He could feel her inner muscles quivering against his arousal. His throat closed, his vision blurred and Omair clenched his jaw against the exquisite sensation, aroused to a point it was almost painful to hold back, and he wanted that delicious, painful sensation to last. He wanted to be with her, inside her, longer.

"Don't. Move," he growled again.

She did, a hard, fast kick of her hips, a salvo in sexual battle. And she laughed huskily as he bucked up into her. But he caught her off guard as he grabbed her shoulder and rolled them both down to the floor of the cave. Omair was careful to land on his good side, pinning her down under him. He heard her suck in her breath as she landed, and in a mock wrestle she opened her legs wider and aggressively clamped her ankles around his lower back, thrusting her hips upward as she did.

He drove down hard into her, pinning her arms up above her head, his good hand holding both her wrists. Memories of Tagua raced through his mind like a disjointed slide show—the way she'd moved in her red dress, the sounds of the jungle outside, the man with snakeskin shoes entering the cantina, the feel of pleasure when he'd realized she was wearing a G-string under that tight red dress, the sensation of her riding naked on top of him, her breasts bouncing...her crying out, head thrown back, as she'd climaxed. It drove him harder, wilder.

And as he thrust into her again she suddenly went still, then cried out, digging her nails into his back, arching her pelvis into him as muscular contractions ripped one after the other in waves through her body. Omair couldn't hold back a second longer. With a powerful, final thrust, he released inside her. She held him tightly as waves of pleasure swept through his body and mind.

Barely able to breathe, he collapsed onto her in hot, sated bliss, rolling carefully onto his good side. She kept her legs wrapped around him as he softened slowly inside her, and even when he had, she kept holding on to him, her breathing going slow and regular.

"Are the rocks cutting into your back?" he asked, his voice thick and husky.

She smiled slowly, and glanced up at him with eyes that looked like a lioness's. "No pain, no gain," she whispered as she gave a mocking little thrust of her pelvis, and Omair felt himself stir again as an aftershock rippled softly through her muscles.

"Your shoulder okay?" she whispered, touching him gently, and the care he saw in her eyes cracked his heart. He couldn't let this woman go. Not now.

He knew her in a way others could not—he'd seen with his own eyes out in this desert what grit she was made of. And he believed he understood what drove her now. In an abstract way he could also understand her loyalty to the identity of her employers—he had to respect that even as he wanted the information.

Faith was his equal in so many ways, his opposite in so many others, and suddenly Omair could see a life ahead with her in it. Faith was a woman who would understand his mission in life, and possibly even support him in it.

Which was absurd.

Because she didn't know him. And she might not care for the plight of his country at all.

A small coil of fear began to unfurl inside him—when had he actually started to want her in this way? What would she say when he told her who he really was?

"My shoulder is fine," he said, quietly. "Sex is a most excellent painkiller."

She laughed, and it warmed his heart.

Tracing the backs of his fingertips along the swell of her breast, the valley of her waist, the rise of her hip, he said, "When was the last time you had a man in your life, Faith?"

Something about her seemed to still.

"Is this your way of asking if I do long-term relationships?"

Omair swallowed. "No," he said quietly. "I'm just curious."

She untangled her legs from him suddenly and edged up onto her elbow, the movement pushing her breasts together, deepening her cleavage. He felt himself stir yet again, and he inhaled deeply.

"What about you, Omair? Strictly a one-night stand kind of guy, given your marriage to your mission—your 'warrior duty'?"

There was a sudden edginess, almost a bitterness to her voice now, and caution whispered through Omair.

"It's by necessity," he said calmly. "But this time... You're different, Faith. I'd like to get to know you better, much better."

She rolled onto her back, and stared in sullen silence up at the black cave roof.

Omair's heart sank and he cursed inwardly. He'd pushed her into a corner, and she'd shut down. He could literally feel her slipping from his grasp. He lay silently by her side in the saunalike darkness, listening to the weather, his eyes closed.

They stayed like that as the hours passed into night, and started ticking toward dawn. Neither slept.

When he heard the wind begin to die and saw the light was changing, he said finally, "Do you think that helicopter went down?"

"I think I hit it where it counted," she replied crisply. "It might have limped along for a few klicks and gone down in the next valley." She sat up suddenly, reached for her sports bra, began putting it on, her mouth tight again.

"What is it, Faith?" he said.

Faith felt her throat tighten. His voice was so sensual, so caring, his black eyes so liquid beneath those long dark lashes. She couldn't bear to look at him. She was powerless under his gaze.

She'd grasped her one last time with him and wasn't sorry about that. She'd needed the human connection, the physicality of making love with him again.

But the longer she stayed in this cave with this man, the more he was going to mess with her mind—and she was terrified of her growing feelings for him.

It could never work.

Faith didn't even know why she was thinking this way.

She just wanted to get to Morocco now, get over that border, start a new life. Away from him, before he sucked her further into his aura.

She yanked on her pants and shirt, and started lacing up her boots. "I can see moonlight," she said. "It'll be clearing soon. When it does I want to go find those camels and get moving."

"Did my questions make you uncomfortable?" he said, sitting up.

"Wasn't that why you kidnapped me—to make me uncomfortable?" she snapped.

"No, it was because you tried to kill me and I still don't know why."

Her irritation, her fear, her need for his affection mixed within her. "How can you say you'd like to spend time with me? I mean, you might know my name but you don't *know* me."

"I think I know more about you, Faith, than most people do. I know what you're made of—I've seen it in this desert, and in Colombia I watched you for many weeks. And you've told me what drives you."

She swallowed against the sharp ball of emotion swelling in her throat. Damn this man. Her eyes pricked with hot emotion and she struggled to tamp it all down before she could speak again.

"If this is just another way to wheedle information out of me I—"

"Faith." The seriousness in his tone, the sudden glint in his eyes, stopped her.

"Why have you stopped trying to learn more about *me?* Why do you no longer want to know my full name, or where I come from? Do you know already? Were you informed of my identity when you placed that call at the wadi—is that why you're not asking?"

"No. And I don't want to know." She yanked her laces tight, and lurched to her feet, moving to stand at the cave entrance.

"Why not?"

She refused to look at him. "Things have changed—"

"*What* has changed?"

"It…it's complicated, Omair. Now that I know I've been set up, I need to disappear, get a new name, start a new life. And I can't take anything from my old one with me. If I know your name…" Her voice choked and she cursed herself.

He got up, came and stood beside her. She could feel his warmth, sense his nakedness. With relief she saw the sky was almost fully clear, the dunes turning silver again under the light of the moon.

"And you feel you have to disappear because these people will keep hunting you?"

"Because of lots of things," she said crisply.

He reached for her hand, but she moved out of his grasp.

"Faith—"

"The answer is no, Omair, I don't do long-term relationships." She held her arms even more defensively over her stomach.

"Why not?"

She spun to face him, eyes glittering. "Speak for yourself—an assassin's life is a lonely one by definition. Maybe that's why I took the job in the first place—I don't know *how* to build a relationship. I've never had practice. I never even had friends!"

"You're afraid of being rejected. Hurt," he said quietly. "Like your father and mother rejected you as a child."

"Oh, that's nonsense."

But he could see in her eyes it wasn't, and it only deepened his compassion, his affection for her.

"It's about survival. I *need* to be able to walk away."

Emotion came dangerously close to the surface and her eyes gleamed. "Maybe I don't want to know who you are because I liked Santiago, and I'd prefer to remember you as him."

"My name is Al Arif," he said. "Sheik Omair Al Arif."

Faith froze.

She stared at him, her entire world tilting dangerously on its axis.

"You mean…" Images from the news eight weeks ago slammed through her brain—the Al Arif royal jet exploding at JFK, renowned neurosurgeon Dr. Tariq Al Arif dying, King Zakir Al Arif battling the resurgence of violence in his kingdom… *Oh sweet hell.*

She lowered herself slowly to a rock, her brain spinning as she recalled the names in his sat phone contact list: Zakir, Tariq, Dalilah. Julie Belard—the name of Sheik Tariq Al Arif's now deceased fiancée.

"Your brother…is king of Al Na'Jar?"

"Yes."

"And you're hunting for the man behind the assassinations of your parents, your older brother, Da'ud, and now of Tariq."

"That is correct."

Her head began to pound. And it hit her—Jacques Sauvage—he was the founder of the Force Du Sable, the private army based off the coast of Africa. Omair had said he'd contracted to the FDS, which was why Sauvage's name must have begun circling in her subconscious and felt familiar when she'd scrolled through his sat phone list.

Faith ran a shaking hand over her hair. It all made sense now. Except one thing—STRIKE had ordered a hit on an Al Arif prince.

This was not possible—that *had* to be a mistake. Al

Na'Jar was an ally of the United States. King Zakir Al Arif had been invited to the UN to talk about how he was trying to ease his kingdom into a democracy. The U.S. was backing him in this endeavor. Senator Sam Etherington, the man everyone believed would be the next president, was even promising very lucrative future oil deals with the small kingdom.

She didn't want to believe Omair. Yet she did. Which meant the impossible.

Oh, God.

She dropped her face into her hands—she was carrying the child of an Al Arif prince. She'd been sent by the United States to kill him. And now her country was out to kill her.

Chapter 11

Faith looked slowly into Omair's eyes.

He was watching her intently, worry etched into his Persian features. He looked like a sculpture, the moonlight filtering into the cave, painting him with silver. Tears filled her eyes. Damn him—she was falling for him, and now that she knew who he was it just made things worse.

Why the United States had tried to assassinate the next in line of succession to the Al Na'Jar throne, Faith had no idea. But telling him, revealing the existence of STRIKE, could topple her own country and make her a red-hot pawn for his kingdom. There'd be no way she could disappear then—even if Omair tried to protect her inside his kingdom. STRIKE *would* find a way to get to her, and kill her. Her baby would die, too.

She held her arms tighter over her stomach, protecting her secret, *her* baby, holding on to that precious feeling she had back at the wadi when it had really hit home that she was going to be a mom.

And another chilling thought struck her: if the Al Arifs learned she was carrying a child of royal blood, a possible heir, they might try to take her baby from her. The laws in that kingdom were not yet in a woman's favor. She needed to disappear, for every reason she could fathom, and fast.

As much as she wanted to help him, she *couldn't*.

"The sky has cleared," she said abruptly. "I'm going to find the camels."

Faith reached for her rifle, but he grabbed her by the arm as she tried to leave.

"Is that what you do when you hear something you don't like? You ignore it? Run away?"

There was hurt in his voice. That made it worse. This was a man with compassion. But he was also ruthless when it came to matters of his kingdom—how ruthless might that kingdom be if they wanted his baby?

"Please, Omair, let me go. We need to find the camels and get moving before daybreak, before another chopper comes."

But his fingers just dug tighter into her arm.

"Faith—you *need* to tell me who wants to kill you, because they're the same people who want me and family dead."

She began to shake inside. "Please, let me go."

"Who sent that chopper?" he demanded.

"I don't know."

"*Who* did you phone from that wadi, Faith?"

"I can't help you. Why don't you just let me be, Omair—"

"Not until I find the people trying to kill my family!"

Part of her soul cracked inside as she was torn by a

need to tell him, help him. The other part of her was desperate to escape, to survive, while she still could.

Her own mother had given up on her by not trying to survive, and Faith sure as hell wasn't going to be her mother. She was going to do whatever it took to survive and save this baby.

"Whoever you called at that wadi sent that chopper, Faith, and you know it."

"I called a voice mail," she answered, very coolly. "I left a message for the agent who brings me jobs. I let him know the deal was off. I guess the message alerted someone, or they were already tracking my GPS systems."

He glared at her and raked his hand over his hair, visibly fighting his anger, frustration, his eyes crackling with fury.

"You could try a little better than this, Faith."

He took her by the shoulder, forcing her to face him. And he seemed even more powerful in his nakedness than clothed. He looked deep into her eyes, hot energy rolling off him in waves.

"I know you are scared, but my family is powerful."

That's what worried her—that they might be powerful enough to take her child, but not powerful enough to protect her from STRIKE.

"I—*we*—can protect you. And I know you care, Faith. I have seen it in your eyes, heard it in your voice. It's been in your actions. I'm falling for you, and I know you feel for me, but we have to trust each other now, if we want to move forward together."

She didn't. As much as she did…she just couldn't.

She jerked out from under his hold and stomped out into the fresh sand drifts, slinging her rifle over her shoulder as she went.

"Faith!" he yelled from the cave.

"I'm going to find the camels," she called out behind her. "Then I'm going to get the hell out of here before they send another chopper."

"Wait!"

Omair cursed violently. Just as he thought he was getting somewhere—this woman was impossible to crack, at least this way. And if she headed out into that sea of sand she was as good as dead—her enemies would see her from miles away. Omair spun around and marched to the back of the cave to grab his clothes.

As he bent down he saw something unusual lying on the floor of the cave where her pants had been. It must have fallen from her pockets. He picked it up and took it to the cave entrance where there was better light.

A pregnancy test?

There was a solid blue line in one of the little windows, and next to the window, printed in English, was the word *positive*.

He shot a glance into the moonlit desert, where her tracks in fresh sand led from the cave.

Faith was pregnant?

Shock slammed through Omair and on the back of it rode a hard wave of sudden rage.

Damn her—she had no right to have kept that secret from him. Being a soldier of fortune was one thing, but taking an innocent child into the field was absolutely another!

Then another thought rushed at him—*what if it was his?*

He'd slept with her eight weeks ago. But he'd used protection—it was not likely. The baby was probably another man's and Omair hated the jealousy that stabbed through him.

Either way, it was not right that she was out here in the desert now. He was going to airlift her to his country where she could get proper medical attention, immediately.

He unbound his arm, yanked on his clothes, thrust his dagger back into his belt, and marched outside. As he climbed the moonlit dune he called Zakir on his sat phone.

"Zakir, I need a helicopter," he said crisply when his brother picked up. "I have an informant. But she's pregnant. I need to bring her to Al Na'Jar where she can be safe. And please, send a medic with the crew." Omair gave their coordinates.

Zakir told Omair he had a military unit currently in training at a base in the Grand Erg. A medical team and chopper could be dispatched from there at once, and arrive within the hour.

Omair signed off, and crested the dune. His mission was now to find Faith and get her back into that cave, until the helo arrived.

He found the two camels before he found Faith in the next valley. She was crouched near the charred and sand-covered wreckage of the chopper, examining something.

The dawn sky was bright but the sun had yet to burst over the horizon and turn the place into an instant furnace. Even so, the temperatures were fierce and the quality of light made Faith's hair gleam in a soft fall about her face.

Omair stilled a moment, struck by her presence of beauty against the charred disaster. And as he led the camels closer, he saw she was bent over the burned and twisted remains of a human body.

Another body hung out of the cockpit. Both wore

flight suits. Both were dark haired, most likely male. There were no immediately discernable markings on the downed craft, but it was one of the smaller, rugged, and easily serviceable models typically sold by the Russians and ideally suited to local conditions. This one had been rigged to function as a gunship. Black market without a doubt, thought Omair, and consistent with MagMo weaponry.

Faith was examining something she'd taken from the body. It glinted gold in her hand.

"It's some kind of medallion," she said as he came up behind her.

He crouched down at her side, pulse quickening. "It's the sign of the MagMo," he said. "I found one just like it on the body of Da'ud's killer in Tagua—he was the bodyguard of the North African arms dealer, which is why I needed your note about the hit. I was there to avenge Da'ud's death."

Her gaze shot to him. "So that's why you needed my note—vengeance?"

"Retribution. Yes. The old way."

The carotid at her neck pulsed fast as she stared at him.

"And since I arrived in North Africa eight weeks ago, I learned that MagMo terrorists have started wearing this symbol as part of the ideology their new leader is spinning. This New Moor claims he and his Maghreb followers are descended from the ancient Sun Clan, a fierce warrior tribe said to have once ruled the Atlas Mountains. The tribe is also rumored to have gone to battle hundreds of years ago with the Al Arif Bedouins over land that now belongs to Al Na'Jar. The New Moor claims the Al Arifs decimated the clan, and he's building it back. He now wants the land back—he claims Al Na'Jar is theirs."

"Is this true, about the battle?" she said.

He shrugged. "It might be, but either way the Moor has given his terrorist organization an identity, a sense of country and ancient purpose when all he really is after is our oil."

"Smart man."

"Very, and dangerous because of it. Far more so than his predecessor. And he's using this same ideology to stir unrest among those of Moorish origin within our own country."

He nodded toward the twisted and burned craft. "It's Russian-made, the kind the dealer I met with in the courtyard sells to MagMo."

"Are you sure?"

He frowned. "As sure as we can be, why?"

"It's…nothing." But she looked suddenly pale, two odd hot spots forming high along her cheekbones. In spite of the heat Omair noticed her skin was dry, and her breathing seemed light and fast.

He needed to get her somewhere cool—she could be showing signs of heat stress.

"I'd bet my life that craft, these people, are MagMo. Especially given the medallion."

"It's not possible," she whispered, glancing at the gold medallion glinting her palm. "They wouldn't work with MagMo."

"What did you say?"

"Nothing." She got up abruptly, determination steeling her features as she reached across him for the rope of the camel he was holding.

"Whoa," he said, jerking the rope out of her reach. "These are my camels."

"Are you serious?"

"Dead serious."

"You abducted me, brought me out here, and won't give me a miserable camel so I can split before these people come back?"

"I cannot allow you to make yourself a sitting duck in a sea of sand, Faith. I'll do better than give you a camel—I'll fly you out of Algeria. I've already sent for a chopper. We'll have you safely in the Al Na'Jar palace before dinnertime."

"What?" she said, a stunned look on her face.

"I called my brother Zakir—he's dispatching transport from a training camp in the Grand Erg as we speak. Their ETA is—" he looked at his watch "—in less than thirty minutes now. We need to go back, wait at the cave in case MagMo comes looking for their downed helicopter." He reached for her arm.

Incredulous, she stepped back from his reach. "I'm not going to Al Na'Jar. I'm going to Morocco. I know someone there who can help me disappear. I *need* to disappear, Omair."

"It's not safe to cross this desert on camel. Your tracks will lead them right to you. I want you out, now. This environment itself is dangerous and no place for a woman in—"

"*Excuse me?* This coming from the guy who bound and rubbed my wrists raw, took my boots, my communications and navigation devices, induced hypothermia, extreme dehydration! Who are you to—"

He took the wand from his pocket.

The words died on her lips and she went sheet-white. "You dropped this. You should have told me, Faith. How far along are you?"

"You had no right—that's private!"

"It was on the cave floor. What were you doing with it out here on a job anyway?"

She grabbed the stick, shoved it into her pocket, turned away and began to trudge up the dune.

"Faith!"

She kept trudging, shoulders wire-tense.

He raced up behind her, grabbed her arm. "Where in hell do you think you're going!"

She whirled around, eyes crackling. "Get your hands off me!"

He met her eyes. "I can't let you do this."

"Why—because you're some prince on a power trip? Because you're used to domineering everyone? You didn't give a damn about hurting me before."

"You were my enemy before," he said quietly. "You tried to kill me—I wanted to try and find out why. And you didn't tell me you were carrying a child. Being a contract soldier is one thing, but you had no right to bring an unborn child into this environment."

"You're judging *me?*" She snorted. "I should have guessed—a prince and a chauvinist. Women have been carrying babies in all sorts of extreme environments since creation—"

"You entered a danger zone by choice, apparently for hard, cold cash. That's different."

Her mouth flattened into a furious line and the hot spots on her cheeks grew redder as her entire body started to vibrate with anger.

"You have no right to judge me!" she snapped back. "You, who takes the law into his own hands, vigilante style, pretending it's some ancient desert warrior code as you avenge the deaths in your family? There are international rules about this sort of thing!"

Omair tamped down a spurt of sudden rage and

chose to sidestep her barb. "You're not endangering that child's life any further. You're coming with me."

"Forget it." She unsheathed her knife, held it out to him.

"Don't be ridiculous, Faith."

She waved the blade. "I mean it. I'm not going to your kingdom."

"It's my country. You'll be safe. We have an army—"

"Yeah, and a revolution, enemies, assassins after your family. Even if I wanted to go, you would not be able to guarantee my safety, trust me. I need to take care of this myself."

"Where is the father of this child, Faith? Who is he? How far along are you?"

"This has *nothing* to do with you, Omair. So please, back off. Just give me a camel and let me go."

Her words were a vicious punch to his gut. And it cut like a knife to think she'd slept with him again, in the cave, while she was pregnant with another man's child. Pressure began to build dangerously in his chest.

"I guess your promiscuity shouldn't come as a surprise," he said, his voice cold.

Hurt, raw, flashed through her eyes. "Oh, that's rich coming from you, Mr. One-Night Stand. What's good for you is not good for a woman?"

"I didn't say that. I just said… Forget it, it was my own error in judgment. I misread you, that's all. I was foolish, or arrogant enough, to think what we just shared in that cave might have been…special."

She glowered at him, hurt sparkling in her eyes, the spots on her cheeks growing redder.

He hurt, too, and felt a fool because of it. Dragging his hand over his hair, Omair tried to temper the dangerous undercurrents of emotion swirling in him.

"And now you want to disappear?" he said, more calmly, his peripheral attention still on her knife. "What about the father of your baby? Does he even know you're pregnant?"

Her eyes flickered. And the sun burst over the horizon, sending color and heat rippling over the dunes, glinting on the blade in her hand. Urgency kicked into Omair. He needed to get her back into the shelter of the cave in case MagMo came looking for its downed chopper before Zakir's team arrived.

"You just found out, didn't you, Faith? That's why you have this test stick with you on the mission. Am I right?"

"Omair, please. It's not your business."

"Are you going to tell him about his child? It's his baby as much as it's yours, Faith. A man has a right to his own child."

"I'm not going to keep it, okay," she said, very quietly. "I can't. So please, back off."

Omair stiffened.

"If you don't want the baby, maybe he does. Maybe he wants to raise his own child. The father has a *right*—"

"Is that what you'd do? Let me carry it to term then just take it? You, who says there is no room for his own children in his life? No room for a wife?"

"This is different. This is—"

"Is what?"

Omair was silent for several beats. "Because it's you, Faith. And if you were carrying my child, I'd…do everything to make it work."

She stared at him, her hands beginning to shake. The desert temperature was climbing fast, and she was looking even more pale save for two hot spots still riding high across her cheekbones.

She lowered her knife slowly, pulled at her shirt. When she spoke again her voice was thin.

"Omair, please, listen to me. I *can't* have this baby. I can't go home—I can't ever see the father of this child again. I need to disappear, or I'm going to die. And my baby will die, too." She pointed to the chopper wreckage. "These people *will* find me."

He took the gap and grabbed her wrist, forcing her to drop the knife to the sand. "I *know* what you are made of, Faith. You don't run—you fight back."

"Oh, you got me wrong, Omair. I do run. You just told me yourself, back at the cave. I run from every bogeyman in my closet. I ran from my father, my home, relationships, and now I'm running from my country, from you. And you're no different, you know that? You hide behind this blood honor thing when really it's an excuse to take the law into your own hands."

"It's necessity, Faith. There's no one else out there who will protect my family. Until I find the man behind all of this, until I get the Moor himself, I won't rest. I can't."

"And meanwhile you use this vendetta to justify your one-night stands, avoid commitment, relationships, being responsible for your *own* children?"

He reeled at her words. They hit hard, they hit home, and they hit deeper than he cared to admit.

"If it was my child," he said simply, "I'd want to know you were in danger. I'd fix it. I'd keep both you and my child safe."

She wouldn't meet his eyes. "Well, it's not your child. So it's not your problem."

And it hit him right there, like a blow to his solar

plexus—he'd *wanted* it to be his. He'd wanted to try to make it work with her before he knew there was a baby, and when he'd found the test he'd been momentarily exhilarated by the thought it could be his. Now he felt as though she was ripping his heart right out his chest.

He also felt in his gut she was lying about this baby— holding something back. He could see it in her eyes, feel it in the tension in her body. She was afraid. She cared for him but was holding back something huge, something that might be putting his entire country in jeopardy.

Desperation mounted in Omair, but he was distracted suddenly by the thudding sound of a chopper in the far distance. Both tensed and glanced skyward. A shimmering metallic speck emerged over the horizon, coming straight for them.

Omair shaded his eyes, squinting into the sun as he watched. It could be either friend or foe, he couldn't tell from this distance.

"Give me the rifle scope," he said as the noise grew louder.

But she already had the rifle in her hands, was raising the scope to her eye.

The helo came in fast, looming in size, noise growing deafening in the hot dawn air.

"Give me the gun, Faith," he demanded, suddenly worried she might shoot an Al Na'Jar chopper down.

But he saw her finger curling around the trigger as the helo neared. It was close enough now for Omair to recognize the distinctive Al Na'Jar emblem on the side of the craft. He lunged out to grab the gun from her as the chopper came over them, downdraft whipping desert sand into a stinging, blinding whirlwind.

She struggled to fight him off as the helo lowered to

the sand, and a stray shot was fired from her rifle, the bullet pinging off the skids of the chopper.

An Al Na'Jar soldier in full gear dropped from the craft to the ground as the skids skimmed sand. He raised his weapon, aiming at Faith as he ran forward in a crouch.

Omair saw the soldier coming at her with singular purpose—he was misreading Faith's intentions, thought she was threatening the prince of his country, shooting at his chopper. The soldier fired just as Omair threw himself at Faith, forcing her to the ground and covering her body with his.

"Hold your fire!" He waved his hand, yelling above the fiercely swirling sand, the deafening roar of the chopper.

The soldier continued to come forward in a predatory crouch, weapon still trained on Faith.

"Hold your fire, dammit!"

The man lowered his weapon.

Omair rolled off Faith, turned her over, while still protecting her from the raging downdraft with his body—sand with this force could cut like glass. But as he moved, Faith's head lolled limply to the side, her mouth open.

The sand under her head was dark with blood.

Chapter 12

Washington, D.C.

Senator Sam Etherington was in a high campaign mood as he stood atop the stairs of the Capitol building fielding questions from reporters gathering below. The U.S. flag snapped crisply in the breeze behind him and he felt tanned and fit—it made for a good photo op, a good backstop to his recently announced tough stance on American justice. A nice subliminal image of a young president-in-the-making who had the country's future and the well-being of families in his virile and capable hands.

Isaiah watched quietly from the sidelines. Sam's cavalcade waited at the base of the stairs, engines running. He had a busy day ahead and the campaign clock was ticking.

Sam pointed to a young reporter with wild dark

hair, a cute gap between her teeth. Her smile was huge
and disarming and her big eyes belied the shark's instinct and political acuity Sam knew lurked beneath.
She tended to take her subjects by surprise, coming
out of left field with her funky clothes, big boots and
short skirt, then she'd hone in for the kill with a razor-
sharp intellect. Sam liked her. He imagined she was
good in bed, too.

"Ms. DiCaprio?"

"Senator, yesterday news broke that MagMo has
claimed responsibility for the Al Arif jet bombing at
JFK. What will an administration with you at the helm
do about it?"

He smiled, liked the fact she'd pointed out he *would*
be the next U.S. president. Cameras clicked and he made
sure they had his best angles.

"The safety of U.S. citizens on home soil is paramount. As this case at the legislature today showed
us we—"

"Will we go after them on foreign soil?" she inter-
rupted from below.

Irritation rippled through him, but he maintained his
broad smile. "We will do everything to ensure safety
of U.S. citizens."

He pointed to someone else, but DiCaprio wasn't
ready to let him go.

"Senator!" she called out. "If you don't mind going
back to the question, one of your campaign cornerstones that was also announced yesterday focuses on
energy and oil from countries like Al Na'Jar. How can
you guarantee this? Al Na'Jar is not an OPEC member
and there are no treaties—"

Sam cut in, his smile turning to steel. "Negotiations
are in the works—"

"MagMo is apparently fueling a rebellion in that country. If they take control, how will you deliver on the campaign promise?"

He stilled inside. The other reporters were taking notes, the cameras rolling.

His secretary stepped in. "If we could keep questions to the matter at hand, which is the overturned conviction of a dangerous criminal who should remain behind bars…"

Sam loosened his red tie, held his hand up to his secretary. "It's all right." He forced a wide smile. "I'll finish this one, and then we move on."

His gaze met DiCaprio's directly.

"I don't know where you're getting your information as to who is fueling unrest in Al Na'Jar, Ms. Di-Caprio, but if you're referencing stories posted on the well-known conspiracy theorist blog, Watchdog, I can refer you to some other sites that might also appeal to your news instincts—there's a particularly good one that covers Bigfoot sightings, and another the Loch Ness monster. Then there's the Roswell site—I shall have my press secretary forward the URLs to you at the *Washington Daily*."

Everyone laughed.

Sam's press secretary stepped forward. "Next question for the senator, and if we could keep to the topic at hand, the senator has an extremely busy schedule…"

Bella DiCaprio pushed quickly through the back of the crowd.

Determination powered her walk to the subway station. No company vehicle for her today. She'd been laid off yesterday due to newspaper cutbacks. And instead of letting the old union-entrenched deadwood go, they'd tossed *her* to the wind.

Her editor, a man she really admired, had given her the spiel—sitting her down and telling her she was one of the best young reporters they'd had, she had the instinct, the credentials, yadda yadda. Fat lot of good it was doing her now. She had rent to pay, a cat to feed.

A white van drew up behind her. The window wound down and a tubby guy with dreads poked his head out the window.

"Bella my belle, want a ride, sweetness?"

"Hey, Hurley," she walked up to the driver's side. "What are you doing here? Is there a pizza joint around here I missed?"

"Where Senator Sam goes, we go." He waffled his eyebrows. "Get in."

She laughed, climbed in.

"Not quite as good as the company car," he said as the van rattled down the highway.

She sighed heavily, slumping back into the seat. "It'll save me transit fare, thanks."

Hurley slid her a glance as he drove. "Newspapers are dinosaurs, Bella. Print media is so over."

"Yeah, well it paid the bills. My rent is due next week."

"Move in with me and Scoob."

She shot him a glance. "You're kidding me, right? I'd go homeless first."

He chuckled, his big hearty laugh comforting her.

She closed her eyes and smiled. "I love you, Hurley, you know that."

"And Scoob?"

"Not Scoob—he's a freak."

"What were you doing back there, anyway?"

She sighed heavily. "I've got a feeling about the

senator and this Al Na'Jar business—I couldn't just let it drop."

"You used your press pass?"

"Sue me."

"Maybe the paper will."

Bella pulled a face.

"Come write for the website."

"Jesus, Hurley, the conspiracy theorist blog? Do you know Senator Etherington just made a mockery of you guys back there?" She wound down the window.

"All the reason to make a mockery of him," he said quietly, eyes fixed on the road.

"Ah, Hurley, I'm sorry—I didn't mean to take a dig at you guys—"

"Citizen journalism—it's the future, Bella. You could break a major news story on the blog and help lead the way."

Bella sank farther into the seat, depression washing over her. She'd hit bottom of the barrel, as low as she could go, but she could *not* go to Watchdog and work for nothing. She couldn't let go of her stories, either.

Sam's team ushered him into his limo, his detail holding reporters with more questions at bay.

"What does that DiCaprio have on me—why is she linking those issues?" he snapped at Isaiah the instant the door to their sealed capsule was shut.

"You're being paranoid, Sam. Those issues link themselves. There will be more questions like hers, from far tougher sources. Deal with it."

Sam inhaled, rubbed the bridge of his nose. "What's the news on our other matter?"

"It's under control."

"What does that mean, exactly?"

Isaiah was silent for several beats. "The operative failed her mission, but we have a location on her. If she's still even alive in that desert, she won't get far without being seen."

Ice washed down Sam's spine. "She's *still* out there?"

Isaiah straightened his sleeve. "It's just a matter of time before we find her. We have a chopper in the air."

"Whose chopper?"

"Don't worry, Sam—leave the details to me. I'm handling this."

"Christ, Isaiah, and you say I'm *paranoid?*"

"I said I'm taking care of it. Our friend knows we're acting in good faith. Once we have them both, we'll tie up the last loose end."

"Her handler?"

"He's the only one who could link this to us."

"And who's going to tie this up?"

"The less you know the better, Sam. Trust me."

Sam scrubbed his hand hard over his face. He was beginning to worry about his choice in Isaiah. Then again there hadn't really been a choice. Isaiah Gold had what it took to get Sam where he needed—zero moral conscience. Isaiah was all about power, and his way to power was through Sam.

"By September this will all be water under the bridge, Sam," Isaiah said very quietly. "You'll have the party nomination officially in the bag. Next step, the Oval Office."

Omair gathered Faith up into his arms and bent into the downdraft as he raced for the roaring chopper.

The instant they were all on board the helo started to lift. The medic pushed Omair aside, taking Faith onto a makeshift stretcher at the back.

"She's been shot!" Omair yelled over the roar of engines, anguish tearing through his chest. "And she's pregnant!"

The medic cast him a look, and moved fast as he checked her pulse and cut away Faith's robe to find the source of the bleeding.

Her body started to convulse.

Omair felt powerless.

He couldn't get angry with the soldier even if he wanted to—the man had done what he thought was right, and he'd done it in the interests of their country.

Someone gave Omair a headset, helped him put it on.

The pilot was speaking into the headset, giving his flight plan and expected arrival time in Al Na'Jar. He was calling for an ambulance to be waiting.

"It's not a bullet wound," Omair heard the medic say in his headphones. Something inside his body stilled.

"Looks like a blade cut through the flesh on the outside of her arm. It's bleeding profusely but superficial." The medic worked quickly to staunch the blood as he spoke.

Omair's heart thudded, and his brain spun. He remembered her waving her knife at him, him grabbing her wrist, forcing her to drop the blade to the sand. The next thing they'd heard the helicopter approaching. And he'd slammed her into the sand to protect her from fire—he must have forced her against the sharp blade lying there.

"Then...why is she unconscious?" he said, voice thick.

"She's coming around," the medic said.

Faith's eyelids fluttered and she moaned, then suddenly tried wildly to push everyone away and get up. The medic strapped her arms and legs down.

"For her safety," he said to Omair. "The knife wound is not my main concern."

Omair glanced at the medic. "What is?"

"Heat exhaustion," he answered, feeling her pulse again and checking her temperature. "It can come on fast and is potentially a life threatening condition if left untreated. The body gets too hot and the brain does not get enough oxygen because of all the blood pooling in the extremities. When this happens individuals can lose consciousness, experience delirium. Shock doesn't help."

Omair rubbed his brow. This was his fault—he'd done this to her.

"The baby?"

"How far is she?"

"I...don't know."

"If she's in the early stages there should be less risk. In later stages it could be more of a problem." He connected a drip with fluids as he spoke.

She moaned, opening her eyes again.

"Faith," he grasped her hand. "You're going to be fine." He tried to smile. "It's just a surface wound, but you have some heat exhaustion. My medic here is taking care of you, and we'll have you at the best hospital in Al Na'Jar in no time—"

"No!" She started to fight against her restraints, her eyes going feverish and wild. "Please...Omair, I can't go there.... Please, don't do this to me!"

In his headset he heard the pilot saying they were about to enter Al Na'Jar airspace.

Omair lurched to the front of the chopper.

"Change direction," he barked. "I want to go north, to Isla del Cheliff in the Mediterranean. You can stay in Algerian airspace."

He returned to Faith.

"My brother Da'ud had a yacht," he explained, stroking hair back from her temple. "I've kept it anchored off a small island in the Mediterranean. We'll go there, put the yacht out to sea, head out through the Strait of Gibraltar into the Atlantic. There'll be no one else on board, just you and me, as long as the medic here clears you. We'll work it all out from there, Faith."

Her body relaxed and her eyes filled with tears. She squeezed his hand hard, and Omair bent down, held her close.

"Why are you doing this for me?" she whispered.

Because, Faith, I think I'm falling in love with you.

"It's the baby, isn't it? And you still want information on who—"

"Shh. Not now."

Suddenly, he realized this was about more than his country. He'd thought for a horrific moment that he was going to lose her, and it made him realize how much he wanted a chance to get to know her better. For the first time in his life, Omair was falling hard for a woman— and she just happened to be an enemy assassin, carrying another man's child.

The irony was a sharp stab to his heart.

Anxiety laced through Faith as she woke in strange surroundings.

She was lying in a large double bed, with silk sheets. The air was cool. Mirrors lined one wall, bookshelves another—expensive cabinetry. Refractions from water danced on the ceiling. She was on some kind of boat.

She sat up sharply, but swayed under a wave of dizziness. Her head was pounding and her arm throbbed.

She was wearing a soft white robe, with nothing

underneath. Faith gingerly edged the robe off her shoulder and touched a clean white bandage around her upper arm. She remembered now, her arm hitting the blade as Omair had forced her to the ground, the pain of it slicing into her. Then there was a gap in her memory.

She glanced around the room. There was an IV drip beside her bed, unattached. She checked her wrist, saw a bandage over her vein from where the drip had been removed. Faith threw back the covers and got up, bracing against the wall for a moment to steady herself.

Once her world stopped spinning, she padded barefoot to the door and stepped out onto a yacht deck. The light outside was gold from late-afternoon sun, and as far as her eye could see, wine-dark sea heaved with white-ribbed swells. *Deep water,* she thought. Land was far away. Bits of memory stabbed back. Omair fighting with her. The helicopter. Feeling sick, very hot, unable to breathe.

"How are you feeling?"

She spun around, glanced up.

He was coming down the stairs from the bridge, his smile devilish, teeth starkly white against his dusky olive complexion. The gold sun painted him bronze and the sea breeze ruffled his dark hair. He was shirtless—loose white cotton drawstring pants hung low on his hips. The muscles of his torso rippled as he moved.

The prince of Al Na'Jar. Handsome as the devil himself.

Faith felt as though she'd slipped through Alice's looking glass into an alternate clean, calm, safe world. Surrounded by sparkling water, lapping waves on a hull, instead of a sea of sand and relentless heat... She could almost forget her stark reality.

"You gave us quite a scare," Omair said, coming

up to her. "But the medic said you're going to be fine. I trust him; he's one of the best. He flies often with Zakir."

"I don't remember...what..." Her hand went to her head.

"Heat exhaustion," he explained. "And you were under severe stress, which didn't help. It could have been a lot worse if we hadn't managed to evacuate you right away." His gaze held hers, shimmering, intense. "You would have died out there, Faith." Then he smiled. "Assassins have nine lives, I think." He took both her hands in his.

"Your pregnancy made you additionally vulnerable. I don't know how to say I'm sorry, Faith. I wish I had known—I would never have taken you out there."

She remembered suddenly—she was pregnant. And he knew.

Her hand went to her stomach and she was reminded she had nothing on under the white robe.

"My clothes?"

His smile deepened. "They needed a wash. There's a closet full of women's clothes in one of the cabins. You can take your pick whenever you're ready."

Her gaze went to the next deck. Above it was a small helipad and higher yet were large white satellite hubs. The lower deck held a row of deep sea fishing rods crafted from what looked like bamboo, wood, cork. There was scuba gear, two Jet Skis, two dive propulsion vehicles, and a Windsurfer strapped to the side—this was a clearly a big money pleasure craft.

"It was my brother Da'ud's yacht," he reminded her, following her gaze. "He liked to entertain and to make his guests comfortable, especially the female ones. Da'ud was playing the field, but really, he was looking for a woman who could be his queen." His eyes turned serious. "He never got that chance to marry, to inherit the throne from my father. He was assassinated off the coast of Barcelona, on this yacht, as he slept, while at the same time my parents were killed in the palace at Al Na'Jar. An attempt was also made on Zakir's life that same night, but he was not in his bed, and this saved him."

"I'm sorry," she said quietly, and the word seemed trite in the face of his tragedies. Somehow being on his dead brother's yacht made Omair's family and his battle feel so much more real, so personal. A pang of guilt stabbed through Faith. What she knew could help him and his country. But it would also seal her and her child's fate.

"Are you hungry?" Omair held his arm out toward a table under an awning. It was laid with fruit, pitchers of juice, ice water. Olives, feta cheese, fish.

"Are we alone on the boat?" she asked quietly, staring at the table, wondering if he'd prepared the food, or if there was staff on board the yacht.

"Absolutely alone." He took her elbow, his touch gentle yet purposeful as he led her to the table. "The doctor did stay with you for a while, monitoring your status. I wanted him to be sure you and the baby were going to be okay. We remained in the Mediterranean until we were certain, then we had him airlifted out. Only the doctor, the pilot, the evac team, and my brother know we're on the yacht, and by now, no one knows our location."

"Where are we?"

He motioned for her to take a seat at the table. "We're in the Atlantic. We sailed through the Strait of Gibraltar early this morning. You can take a look on the navigation systems later if you want to see our exact coordinates."

Faith sat, feeling surreal. "How long was I out?"

He smiled again, warmly, his eyes liquid. She hadn't seen him like this—in a truly relaxed mode, in quiet luxury. He seemed the prince he was.

And he was formidable. All power, yet with grace.

It came slamming back suddenly, how she'd lied to him about the baby—what he said he'd do if it was his. Her heart began to race all over again.

"You slept for almost two days." Omair poured ice water into a frosted glass as he spoke, adding a fresh sprig of mint before handing the glass to her. "Your system needed it. Intravenous fluids and electrolytes helped replenish you."

Faith drank deeply, never so grateful for an abundance of water and ice. She closed her eyes, the sheer passage of their recent journey, the weight of it, sinking in, the fact she was going to be a mom. The fact she could never go home. Nerves began to whisper again—what was she going to do now?

"Don't you want to eat?"

"I'm not hungry."

He opened his mouth to protest but she spoke first. "And don't go saying I need to eat for two."

A smile toyed with the corners of his beautiful mouth, a genuine warmth in his black eyes.

Guilt burrowed deeper into Faith as another memory came back to her suddenly—the look of sharp disappointment on his face when she'd told him the baby was someone else's, the disapproval in his eyes when he thought she'd slept with him while carrying another man's child.

Conflict swirled through her chest.

"Shall I show you around the yacht, then?"

"You're not going to start pressing me for details on who I work for?"

"That's not why I brought you here, Faith."

"I wasn't born yesterday, Omair," she said quietly. "Maybe you think you'll get more from me via a soft approach."

He rammed his water glass down on the table, anger flickering into his dark eyes. Then he held still a moment, visibly tempering the passion that seemed to be simmering just under his skin.

"Yes, Faith, I want the information," he said very quietly. "It might save my family and my country. If you want to withhold that information for fear it will bring danger to you and your baby—I fully appreciate that. But I *can* protect you, Faith. I can make your enemy go away if you only tell me who it is."

"How?"

"Go after him, and get rid of him."

"It's that simple?"

"That simple."

He had no idea.

"And then?"

"And then you will be free to go home, and be with the father of your child—become a family, should you so choose."

Faith reeled.

She turned away sharply, and glared pointedly at the ocean, wishing she could make all the bad stuff vanish and just be with him on this yacht forever in some kind of suspended reality. The warmth, the passion, the admiration she felt for this man was overwhelming. And the guilt was deep.

Omair *should* know that the U.S. was in collusion

with MagMo to destroy him. The knowledge would help him protect his country. But once she'd told him, once the truth about a top-secret U.S. assassin squad came out, it was going to be much harder for her to hide, if not impossible, to disappear.

STRIKE—hell, the entire U.S. military and intelligence machine—was going to come after her in ways he couldn't even begin to imagine, and he alone would not be able to stop them.

She had no guarantee either that Zakir's regime wouldn't use her as a political pawn, putting her right in the crosshairs.

"Why would you do this, Omair?" she said, still staring out at the ocean. "Why would you go to great risk to eliminate my enemies, keep me safe, just so I could be with another man?"

He inhaled deeply.

"I watched you sleeping in that bed, Faith, the same bed in which Da'ud was killed. I thought about the life growing inside you, and it struck me how short a human life really is, and I thought about what makes that life special—family, babies. Love. And while my mission has always been about family—my brothers, sister, vengeance for the assassination of my parents—something you said in the desert got to me. You said I was running from my own fear of commitments, and it struck me that maybe I did want a better balance, that maybe I *could* have more. And if I can't have it with you, I want to at least give you the chance to have it with the baby's father. I want to give you time to think things through before you make a choice from which you can't return."

Faith got up and walked to the railing, gripping it tight. Wind, soft and rounded and filled with salt, washed over her face. She tried to breathe, tried to stop the shaking inside her.

He came up behind her, placed his hand on her shoulder.

Raw emotion tore through her at the sensation of his touch and she fought the urge to lean into him.

"Faith—look at me."

She wouldn't, *couldn't*. She clenched the railing tighter, staring out to sea. "Don't do this. Please don't lie to me like this. I have information and you want it and…" She wavered, struggling to keep her emotions in check. "I don't deserve this, Omair."

"If it were my child," he said quietly, "even if you didn't want it, I would raise it on my own. And if you wanted to be with me, we could raise it together. I'd be there for you every step of the way."

She knew what he was doing. He was opening hypothetical doors, because he still believed it just might be his. And Faith ached to trust him—to lean into his words, to lean into his arms, to feel safe, to go through one of those doors and tell him.

"You'd really give up your life, your mission, to hunt down the Moor, to care for a wife and baby?" She snorted gently. "It goes against everything you've said, and are."

"No, I would not give up my mission. You'd become a part of it. You'd *become* my life, my family. You'd be part of what I was defending."

"Why?" she said hoarsely.

He turned her to face him, compassion liquid in his dark Persian eyes, a soft ferocity of purpose in his features, a gentle strength in his hands.

"Because, Faith, I think I'm falling in love with you. I believe you could come to love me, too."

Tears flooded down her face, no holding back the tide now.

"No one has ever said that to me," she whispered, wiping her face. "Apart from my mother."

"Said what?"

"They love me."

He took her face in his hands, kissed her so powerfully yet tenderly, it made her heart break. She pushed him back, looked up into his eyes.

"You don't even know me, Omair," she said softly against his mouth.

"Then let me."

And he kissed her again, deeper, holding her tight on the deck as the sun sank in a golden ball to the silent swells.

Faith pulled away from him suddenly, dragging her hands through her hair, tormented with the weight of the situation she was in. She'd known the drill when she'd signed on as a government assassin. She understood the sticky issues around "retirement" from the unit.

She was a soldier and loyal to a fault. Political and military decisions were not hers to make—her job was to follow orders. Still, she could not fathom why STRIKE would work hand in hand with a known terrorist group like MagMo.

Where had that decision come from—the Pentagon? CIA? Or could it be that STRIKE as an organization had gone rogue itself—its very secrecy making it vulnerable to exploitation. If that was the case it *should* be exposed.

The U.S. electorate should know their military was working with the same terrorist organization that had just tried to launch an unprecedented biological suicide

attack on their country. She swore to herself. No matter
what she did, if she spoke, she would die.

Even disappearing with a new ID was not a fail-safe.

But maybe Omair *could* help hide her, at least until
she had their baby. Then her child wouldn't have to
die with her. At least their child would have a father if
STRIKE got her.

Bottom line—she could no longer lie to this man.

Nine to ten months. That was all she needed. If she
could make him promise not to use—or go public—
with the information she was about to give him for nine
to ten months minimum, she could save their child.

She inhaled deeply and turned to him. "I'm a soldier,
Omair. I have a deep loyalty to my country and what I'm
about to tell you is going to betray that loyalty. But…"
She wavered. "I…I owe it to you, too, to tell you."

His body went taut and his eyes narrowed sharply.

"I'm a government assassin with a black ops hit unit
called STRIKE."

A muscle at his jaw began to pulse. His neck was
tight.

"What government?"

"The United States."

He reeled visibly, but remained silent.

"We're the ultimate NOCs—screw up and you're
cut loose. Become a loose end, they send a cleaner. I
screwed up in Tagua, Omair. The hit on Escudero was
supposed to be a surgical strike, no collateral damage.
The weapons were supposed to continue with the North
Africans to the Sahara, and the CIA was to track them
to the buyers. But you took my note and blew my job
apart. After eight weeks in debriefing, however, they
told me I was cleared."

She paused, the thunderous intensity on his face unnerving her.

"Maybe I was actually in the clear for a while—I don't know. But you told me that four weeks ago a contact of yours in the States tried matching my DNA profile in government systems. That would have sent a computer alarm directly to STRIKE, showing someone was onto one of their operatives, and I'd have been immediately targeted to be scrubbed." She snorted softly. "Basically I was toast from the moment I met you. You...you have no idea what a role you've played in changing my life since I made the biggest mistake of all—sleeping with you. If I hadn't—"

"Do you understand what this means?" A dark electrical energy quivered off him in waves. "It means the U.S. sanctioned my murder."

"Or the unit has gone rogue."

He spun around, then swung back to face her. "And they're working with MagMo, the same organization trying to overthrow my country?" He cursed. "And there we thought the country was an ally? What does the U.S. want—our oil? Will they back a MagMo government in Al Na'Jar?"

"I have no idea what's behind the MagMo–U.S. alliance, Omair. I just follow orders and I don't know how the decisions come down. Our unit is highly compartmentalized for security reasons. I don't even know who the other operatives are unless I am assigned to work with one. My instructions come from my handler, and him alone. I have no idea who he answers to, and when I go into debrief, it's nameless military and psych personnel I deal with, and never see again." She felt exhausted suddenly.

"I was a good soldier, Omair. I was a good assassin,

but you made it personal. You gave me a conscience. I can't keep this from you anymore, no matter the consequences."

He clamped his large hands over the deck railing, his arm muscles pumped, his jaw tight. "So your handler gave a direct order to kill me—he was the one who said I was Faroud bin Ali."

"Yes."

"What is his name?"

"Omair, you can't—"

"*What* is his name!"

She took another deep breath—this was it. This was the line in the sand and she was crossing it.

"Travis Johnson. I called him from the wadi, that's when the chopper came after me."

"How did he know I was meeting with the Russian in Algiers?"

"Hell knows—I was told the man was CIA, not Russian."

"If STRIKE is colluding with MagMo, this Travis Johnson could have been tipped off by the Algerian MagMo cell that I'd be in that courtyard. The Russian could have looked into my background and leaked the information to them." He swore bitterly. "But why would the Moor use the U.S. to hit me?" He turned to her, took her hands in his.

"Faith, thank you for telling me. I need to contact Zakir at once." He started to move toward the bridge.

"Omair, *wait!*"

He swung back to face her and saw the light in her amber eyes was gone, a look of resigned acceptance on her face. And Omair kicked himself—he'd made her a promise, to keep her safe. And he saw now the scope of what she'd been struggling with, the reason she'd wanted to disappear.

She'd just betrayed her country. For him.

He came up to her, every molecule in his body humming fiercely with a passion for this incredible woman. He grabbed her and kissed her hard. Then holding her at arm's length he said, "I see why you were worried, Faith. But whatever Zakir does with this new position on the U.S., he *will* keep you out of it. You will *not* become a pawn. I promise you that."

"Omair…" Her voice was strange. "You can't keep me safe for long. Irrespective of what I've just told you, they're going to keep looking for me. Travis knows I'm onto him. There was no safe house, no evacuation plan. I was meant to die after I shot you. I ask just one thing." She met his gaze.

"I beg of you, please, do not go public with this information until I've given birth to our child."

Chapter 13

Omair heard the words.

Our child.

They were like a bolt of powerful electricity straight to his chest, and a dark and dangerous passion swelled so fiercely in him that he felt twenty times his size. He struggled to stay calm.

"Are you sure?"

She wiped her nose. "I haven't slept with anyone else in almost two years. I...I was sick with a bug in Colombia, perhaps that's why the pill didn't work. And condoms obviously have their limitations."

"It's *mine?*"

She nodded, smiled, tentatively.

He just stared at her beautiful face, not quite able to absorb her words. He was going to be a father!

He threw back his head, closed his eyes for a second. He felt his family, his mother, father, the entire universe smiling down on him.

The irony, the absurdity of it all, was not lost on him. They'd met to kill, fallen in lust, then love, and now they'd created *life*.

A team.

This woman who could be his equal, who could understand who he was and what he did, was *his*. If she'd have him.

He cupped the back of her head, drew her close, and leaned in for a kiss. It was gentle, beautiful, and he opened her robe, placed his hands on her warm tummy, and he thought nothing in this world could be more perfect than this.

He pulled back suddenly. "Come!" he said grasping her hand. "I want to show you something."

Omair led Faith into the salon. His energy was palpable and his eyes shone. And the relief, the love she felt for this man right now was indescribable. With her hand in his she suddenly felt invincible.

He brought her up to a paneled wall on which a series of photographs had been mounted. He pointed to one.

"That's my brother Zakir, beside Nikki, his queen."

Faith stepped forward to study the photo more closely. Nikki was wearing a diaphanous veil, her hair covered. Around them children of various ages played, all dark-skinned. Faith had read that Zakir's queen was of Nordic origin and she was surprised to see that Nikki covered herself even in a family photo.

"Those seven are their adopted children." Omair smiled. "All were war orphans, children of violent pasts. Nikki saved them."

"I didn't know."

"She used to be a renowned Chicago eye surgeon, married to a man who was, at the time, a top Chicago lawyer. They had two beautiful toddlers."

Faith shot him a glance. "I thought she came from Norway."

He placed his arm around her shoulders. "There's a reason I'm telling you this, Faith. It's a family secret. It's why Nikki doesn't leave Al Na'Jar, and it's why she always wears a veil in any public photo. I'm trusting you with this secret because you trusted me with yours. And I believe in my heart you will never hurt Nikki by talking about this, because she was like you."

"An assassin?"

He laughed. "No, she wanted to hide. She fled from her very powerful and abusive husband who is now about to become one of *the* most powerful men in the United Sates."

A chill washed over her skin. "You can't mean—"

"Senator Sam Etherington."

Her mouth opened, her brain racing.

Sam Etherington hailed from Chicago and had a legal background. His first wife—Dr. Alexis Etherington, an eye surgeon—drove off a bridge with their twins, killing them. Dr. Etherington spiraled mentally after that, eventually losing her medical license. The media raked her through the mud over it all, and then she just disappeared. It was a huge mystery at the time. The senator had her declared dead in absentia years later. He'd since remarried and had two more children.

"Sam Etherington tried to kill his wife, Faith. He hired a hit man who ran her off an icy bridge. Then he tried to blame his wife for the deaths of their children."

"I remember the accident," she whispered. "It was all over the news, particularly because Sam was running for a senatorial seat at the time." She shot him a look. "Nikki is *Alexis?*"

He nodded. "She fled her country under very difficult circumstances, and she came to Africa where she could save children because she hadn't been able to save her own. For five years Nikki worked as a volunteer nurse at a mission orphanage in one of the most remote and hostile regions of the northwest Sahara. But when rebels attacked the mission, killing everyone, she was forced to flee into the desert with a small surviving band of orphans. When she unwittingly crossed into Al Na'Jar in the middle of the last coup attempt, Zakir took her in. Zakir himself was struggling with the fact he'd just become king of a country in chaos. And he was going blind. Nikki became his guiding force, and he fell in love with her. He did everything to protect her from Sam, Faith. Like I will protect you from STRIKE."

"Omair, if this news about Nikki gets out now, it could scuttle the senator's run for the White House," she said. "It could send him to prison."

"It won't get out. Because protecting Nikki's anonymity, her secret, her new life is paramount to all of us."

"Even if it means the senator—the future president— gets away with murder?"

Omair nodded. "Unless Nikki wants different. I helped build her new identity with my FDS contacts. Together Zakir and I gave her a past, and a future. This is how much I—*we*—can we can do for you, Faith. We can build you a new life."

He turned to her. "If you will let me."

But before she could say another word, a pinging alarm sounded urgently from the bridge.

Omair's body went rigid.

"That's the satellite surveillance system," he said quietly. "We've got company."

* * *

Faith ran after him as he took the stairs to the bridge two at a time, the setting sun bronze on his torso. Her mind reeled with the information he'd just given her, but there was no time to think about it. He'd pulled up a live satellite view of their location, and two crafts were rapidly approaching their yacht in a pincer format—one coming from the east and one from the south.

"High performance jet boats," he said. "Military class."

Faith's pulse started to race.

The boats slowed suddenly in unison, and stopped.

"They've stopped just outside our radar range."

"They think we can't see them?"

He nodded. "My bet is they don't know we have military-standard satellite surveillance on board, and that we can see them from the air," he said quietly, watching the boats. "The Al Na'Jar military uses geo-stationary satellites to produce very detailed imagery of the western Sahara and coastal regions. Zakir acquired the technology for Al Na'Jar after receiving threats from rebels with base camps in the desert. The yacht has access to it."

"What do you thing they're doing, laying low until dark?"

He nodded. "They'll probably come in quietly, surprise us."

Omair calmly powered up the yacht engines, began to move slowly south, then changed direction suddenly.

The boats adjusted their positions accordingly, maintaining their speed, staying the same distance away.

"They know we're here—they're locked onto us. They must also be using a satellite system, which likely means military connections."

"You said no one apart from your brother and the evac team knew we were on this boat."

Omair frowned, moistened his lips. Either they'd been tracked somehow, or worse, there was an internal breach in Zakir's team. The sun was already beginning to dip into the sea and once it got fully dark, this satellite system—and theirs—would have limitations.

He zoomed closer in on the satellite image.

"I can make out five people in total," he said, studying the boats. "Could be more below deck." He reached for his encrypted sat phone and called Zakir.

"We've got company. Two high-performance crafts, minimum five occupants, just outside of radar range. Looks like they're going to move when it's dark in an effort to surprise us. We're going to need backup." He hesitated. "Who knows about this, Zakir?"

"The extraction team. So far that's all."

"We might have a breach," Omair said quietly in Arabic. "Whoever you deploy for backup, keep them in the dark, a need-to-know basis only, and *if* we get through this, I want everyone to believe Faith died in the attack."

"You *better* get through it, my brother," Zakir replied. "Nikki went into labor an hour ago, and when those twins come out into this world, they're going to want to meet their uncle, understand?"

Emotion tightened Omair's chest. He glanced at Faith. He wanted to share their news with Zakir. But now was not the time to tell his brother that he, too, was going to be a father.

Signing off, Omair said to Faith, "Best-case scenario is air support from Al Na'Jar within three hours—they'll need to get through Moroccan airspace to the coast, and then fly over the ocean." He zoomed the image out as he spoke.

"The closest mainland is the coastline south of Casablanca to the east, over here." He pointed. "The next closest land is the island of Funchal, there to the west of us."

"And miles of nothing but ocean in between," Faith said. "The sun will set before reinforcements reach us." She began to pace, tying her robe closed. Then she whirled back to face him.

"You've got dive gear on board—I saw it."

"What are you thinking?"

"That we're not going to get backup before those jet boats move in. Either they're going to blast us right out of the water with RPGs, or they're going to board with weapons. Either way we're outgunned and outnumbered. Once they start to move closer they risk us picking them up on radar, even in the dark, so I figure the most efficient way for them is to come in at high speed, and fire some kind of handheld missile. Boom, we're gone."

"What do you suggest?"

"The only way for us to survive is to go underwater, below the boat. Way below. At night they won't likely pick this up on satellite. And if for some reason they don't try and blast us out and come aboard instead, we can surface, come over the backs of their crafts, and use the element of surprise."

She moved to the door. "I'm going to get the scuba tanks. I saw them on the deck—"

But he grabbed her, his face going serious. "Faith, you can't do this."

"Of course I can, I've worked scenarios like this before."

"No, I mean, I can't allow you to do it. You're pregnant. Diving is not safe, the fetus absorbs as much nitrogen as the mother and can't get rid of it."

She hesitated.

"Are…you sure?"

"There've been no official studies done, but the consensus is that depth and pressure increase risk to the fetus. This information I got from a medic with the FDS—we had a military diver who got pregnant, and they made her take maternity leave as soon as they knew."

She dragged her hands over her hair, going suddenly pale. "Dammit, Omair, you've just given me all the reason in the world to live, to change, to try something new. I'm used to being in control—I can't just sit here!"

Conflict tore through Omair.

He didn't want to risk harming his child, but she was right, their chances were not good above water. Then it hit him. He jerked back, holding her at arm's length.

"The diver propulsion vehicles! They're like underwater jet skis—the DPVs can be set to shut off at a predetermined depth. It's not breathing the compressed air from the tanks that's dangerous, Faith, it's depth. We could use the scuba tanks, stay no more than eight feet below the surface and travel out from the yacht. If we leave right now we can put in some good distance before nightfall. Go get suited up!"

Omair quickly called Zakir, outlining their strategy. "We'll set a direct westerly course toward the island of Funchal."

"The batteries on the DPVs won't last that long," Zakir replied. "You won't reach land."

"We'll take the individual survival rafts with us, inflate them once the coast is clear. We'll need long line evacuation from the ocean when the helos get here. The rafts have personal locator beacons that are activated upon inflation. And I'll have my sat phone."

He gave Zakir the yacht coordinates.

"I've got you on satellite now, I can see where you are." He paused. "Be careful."

"The twins?"

"Not yet. By the time we pluck you from the ocean, they'll be waiting for you. Don't disappoint Nikki, Omair."

Omair heard the subtext and worry in his brother's words.

"I won't." Omair signed off, raced to the next deck. Faith was pulling a wetsuit over her naked body. He stalled for a moment at the sight of her full bare breasts as she zipped the suit over them.

"Not exactly comfortable," she said. "But no time to find a bathing suit."

Omair's chest tightened. He realized now why she'd looked softer, more feminine to him. It was the pregnancy. Her breasts were full because of it. She glowed with it. A powerful protective fire began to rage in him. *Nothing* in this world was going to stop him from marrying her, being with her for the rest of his life—as long as she would have him.

He suited up himself, tested the scuba tanks. She grabbed a pair of fins and shrugged on her tank as he checked the charge on the DPVs. He zipped his phone into a waterproof pouch, gave her a diving knife, and he took a spear gun. They each slung a canister containing a single person inflatable life raft across their chests.

Within fifteen minutes they were bobbing quietly in the slowly heaving swells alongside the yacht as the sun sank below the horizon. They waited a few moments longer for full dark, when they'd no longer be visible via satellite from the sky.

Omair met her eyes through the dive mask. She gave a thumbs-up, nodded.

And down they went. LCD displays showed depth, and at a mere eight feet they leveled out below the surface. Bubbles streamed behind them as they put the DPVs to full speed, using their bodies and fins like dolphins to steer.

Faith's hair flowed white behind her and Omair smiled around his mouthpiece—she was his killer mermaid. And if this worked, if the yacht was blown up, it was the perfect time for her to vanish from her old world for good, and enter his new one.

They traveled for almost an hour in the mystical darkness of the ocean, tiny lights from their DPVs throwing phosphorescence in their wake. Through the surface above they could see the glimmer of stars. After another hour of traveling, Omair flicked his light, their sign. She killed her engine, and their vehicles floated slowly to the surface as they held on.

They bobbed on the surface in the dark for maybe twenty minutes before an explosion sent shock waves through the water. About ten miles out an orange glow lit the sky. They watched it fade over time as pieces of Da'ud's yacht burned and drifted down to Davy Jones's locker. No one would know they weren't on that boat.

When the fire in the distance had died, and there was no sign of any jet crafts heading their way, they inflated their personal survival rafts.

The U-shaped design of the rafts allowed for easy entry from the water, and with the sea anchor deployed, the rafts floated facing downwind so the canopies could remain unzipped.

Omair held on to Faith's raft as they bobbed in the dark. Their bodies were submerged below the water-line, which was comfortable but cold.

After yet another hour, the cold grew bitter. Faith began to shiver, but it didn't matter. She reached out for Omair's hand, squeezed. Even adrift in the ocean in the dark and cold she'd never felt safer. And in the darkness like this, she sensed they were three, a family. Them against the world on the ocean of life.

"Will you marry me, Faith?" he said suddenly out of the darkness.

Surprise rippled through her. Then she laughed, but she quieted as she felt the weight of his sincerity in the following silence.

She glanced at him, his black eyes glittering in the shadows of his orange life cocoon.

"I never dreamed about getting married," she said, "but if I had, not in my wildest fantasies could I have imagined being proposed to in his-and-her life rafts in the middle of the Atlantic Ocean."

Silence descended, apart from the slap of water against their rafts.

"You didn't answer," he said after a while.

"I think you know the answer," she replied quietly. "I was destined to be a part of your life, one way or another, from the day I saw you in that Tagua cantina, *Santiago*."

He chuckled. "So that's a yes?"

"It's a maybe. Yes would make it too easy for you."

He yanked her raft toward him, reached over and kissed her.

They fell silent again, and time seemed to stretch to eternity as they watched the heavens move above them. Faith supposed that if they did die out here together, it would still be a good ending, considering her life, and all the other ways she could have gone. She started to drift inside her mind, shivering in the cold.

"Why'd you never dream of marriage?"

She pulled herself back into focus. "Let's just say my father and mother weren't exactly great ambassadors for the institution of marriage and family life." She was unable to keep the bitterness from her voice.

"They made me see marriage was a farce, a lie, and that behind smiling families and little white picket fences, there lurked dark things you didn't share with neighbors." She paused. "I hated them both because of it."

"Yet you brought a damaged photo of them on your mission—why?"

Memories rolled through Faith's mind. She listened to the small slaps of water and she felt something nudge her below, at first soft, then hard, maybe a fish. She looked up at the sky again, noting the passage of the stars. Help better come soon or they were going to end up as shark bait.

"Why the photo, Faith?" he repeated.

"I don't really understand why I brought it, Omair," she said eventually. "I've always tried to block my childhood out, and when I signed up with STRIKE, I threw everything from my past away, but that one photo of my mother holding me... I couldn't let it go. I put it in a safe deposit box, and when I suspected I was pregnant, just before flying out on the Algiers mission, I found myself at the bank looking for that photo. It was like I needed to understand, accept something."

"That you loved your mother. That you needed her."

Unexpected emotion seared into Faith's eyes.

"Jesus, Omair. Did anyone ever suggest you become a shrink instead of a mercenary?" she snapped.

He laughed softly in the dark.

"Reading human nature is one of the most powerful tools of an assassin. You know that, Faith. So, *did* you love her?"

"I told you I hated her. She was weak."

"But she's the reason you became strong?"

"I don't want to be her," Faith said. "To the outside world my father was a war hero but inside the house he abused the bottle, abused her, abused me. Outside the house we pretended nothing was wrong, went to church on Sundays, smiled and shook hands with everyone. I started to hate my mom for not even trying to stand up to him. And then she took her life, just gave up, leaving me alone with my dad."

"She didn't protect her child."

"No. Nor herself."

"She must've been having a really rough time to do what she did."

Faith blew out a breath and shivered. "I guess." She was silent awhile. "I hated myself, too. For not being able to help her." Her voice grew thick. "Because I did love her," she said very softly, and tears filled her eyes. "I just…didn't understand. I hurt. And…I never wanted to hurt like that again, Omair. Ever."

He squeezed her hand.

Faith closed her eyes and inhaled deeply. Admitting it was powerful, cathartic and it brought years of pent-up pain to the surface.

"I was just so angry, young, afraid when I ran away. I vowed never to be like either of them. I was bounced around foster homes, joined the army at first opportunity. The military became my family, STRIKE became my way of hitting back."

"And it led you here, Faith. To me. To us."

God, she loved this man.

"And I won't be my mother," she said. "I *will* protect my child."

"*We* will. Our child."

They saw the chopper lights in the sky before they heard the sound.

Omair took his sat phone from the waterproof pouch and dialed.

"It's them!" he said as his call was picked up. Faith released the emergency flares. They glowed like fiery pink parachutes in the sky, guiding the helicopters in.

Washington, D.C.

In the early dark hours of a stormy Saturday morning, Sam got the call from Isaiah.

"It's done. They're gone."

Sam sat bolt upright in bed. *"Both?"*

Rain lashed against his bedroom window, thunder cracked.

"They were both on board when the yacht was hit with RPG fire. No one could have survived that explosion."

Sam inhaled slowly, deeply. "And now we pray that she didn't speak first."

"It doesn't matter—he's gone. No one can prove anything."

"I still want to seal our loose end in D.C."

"Johnson?"

"Yes."

"I should have it taken care of within the next ten days."

Sam killed the call, lay back in his bed, and slowly he smiled. He could taste it—the Oval Office. The power. It was an aphrodisiac.

"Who was that, honey?" his wife asked sleepily next to him.

"Just some campaign news."

"Good news?"

"Very good news."

She turned to him and they made hard love as the storm raged outside.

Two days later, Kingdom of Al Na'Jar.

Omair, his arm proudly around Faith's shoulders, led her into the green room of the summer palace in the north mountains. The air was cooler at this higher elevation, and it was an ideal place for Nikki and the brand-new twins to spend the hot months.

The babies had been born early and were considered a miracle after Nikki had been told she'd never have children again, let alone more twins. Faith had heard of childless couples suddenly able to conceive after adopting. Perhaps it was the hormones of happiness that did it. But after adopting seven war orphans, the king and queen were now parents of biological fraternal twins, a boy and a girl.

As they entered the room, Zakir was holding one of the babies. Nikki knelt by his side, guiding his hand over the newborn's tiny features as the blind king committed them to memory.

Faith stilled in the doorway and stopped Omair with

her hand. She didn't want to intrude, and for a moment they watched silently from the sidelines.

King Zakir was taller than he looked in photos, and a slightly leaner version of Omair, but he had the same dusky skin, blue-black hair, aquiline features, dark almond-shaped eyes. Except his eyes stared straight ahead, sightless, as his beautiful fingers explored the line of a tiny newborn nose, rosebud lips. Zakir smiled at what he was touching and Faith's heart clutched. She reached for Omair's hand.

Nikki looked up, saw them.

"Hey," she said, getting up, a warm smile lighting her eyes. "Zakir, Omair and Faith are here."

Zakir handed the baby back to the nurse, his movements sure. And as he stood, his two slender salukis immediately surged to his side.

Resting his hand on the head of the tallest hound, he came confidently forward, his powerful stride befitting of a monarch.

He reached out his hand.

Faith took it in both of hers.

"It's good to finally meet you, Zakir," she said.

"And I cannot tell you how happy I am that you're making an honest man out of our renegade brother." He held on to her hands for a moment, staring into space over her shoulder. But in his touch she could feel his connection, his warmth, his sincerity.

"Congratulations, Faith, on your news," he said quietly. "And welcome to our family."

Emotion choked in her throat.

Zakir smiled then slapped his younger brother on the shoulder. "Come, you two… Come meet the newest Al Arif additions."

Faith took a step forward, not quite able to absorb what a powerful impact the king's words had on her.

Welcome to our family.

And she realized just how badly she'd wanted to belong to one. Her whole life she'd been running from the very thing she'd craved—a sense of belonging, and to be loved.

It had sent her down a hard, cold and solitary path, which ironically had led her here, to a most unusual extended family of incredible warmth, loyalty, honor. She glanced at Omair. He was making her a part of it without for a moment taking away her freedom. Or strength.

"Do you want to hold them?" Nikki asked Faith.

"Me?"

Nikki laughed. "It'll give you practice. Looks like you could use some."

A chair was pulled out, and the tiny infant twins were placed in Faith's arms. A sense of awe washed over her. They were so perfect, so small. She glanced up at Omair, tears in her eyes, joy in her heart.

"It suits you, Faith." He leaned down. "I'm still going to make you marry me," he whispered near her ear.

"Just no picket fences, okay?"

He laughed.

"In the desert? I don't think so." And Omair kissed her. Over the scent of the babies, his heart was almost bursting with love and a new sense of purpose.

Family had new meaning for him now. Deeper than he could ever imagine.

And he would defend it to the death.

Epilogue

Washington, D.C., five days later.

Travis Johnson was six-three, dark-skinned and all rippling muscle. He walked as if he owned the space around him.

Dressed in a black balaclava, pants, leather jacket and gloves, Omair watched from the shadows in the dark and empty underground parking garage as Johnson strode toward his parked SUV.

As he came up to his vehicle, Johnson got his keys out from his pocket and pressed the remote. The alarm blipped as it disarmed. But before he could open the passenger door Omair lunged from the darkness and body-slammed him against the wall, pressing the blade of his jambiya to the man's throat.

Omair was doing this for his wife-to-be, his child, his family, his country—his mission hadn't changed, just grown in a way that had made him whole, and even more dangerous than before.

Because now he had a lot more to lose.

"Do you know who I am?" he whispered in Johnson's ear.

Johnson tried to turn his head to look but Omair hit him square in the face. Johnson's nose made a crunching noise and started to bleed. Raw fear entered his eyes.

"My name is Sheik Omair Al Arif," he whispered through his mask as he pressed his dagger tighter against Johnson's neck. The man's body went wire-tense.

"I want to know who ordered Faith Sinclair's last hit."

Sweat began to bead over Johnson's brow.

"I don't know what you're talking about," he said.

Omair whipped out a smartphone, pressed a button, and held it in front of the man's bleeding nose. "This is live, and this your wife and daughter."

Johnson stiffened at the image on the phone of his wife and child walking through a mall.

"I know how important family is, Johnson, and I have people watching them right now, waiting for my orders. Do you want your wife to die? Do you want your daughter dead, too?"

"Okay," he ground out through his teeth, eyes watering. "What do you want from me?"

"The name of the person who instructed you to send Faith after me."

"It was my decision alone." His voice was hoarse.

Omair pressed the dagger harder against the carotid pumping furiously in Johnson's neck. Skin broke and blood began to dribble to his collar.

"I don't believe you really want to take this one for the team, Johnson. Your orders came from higher up. I want the name of the man who ordered me dead or I give my men the order to pick up your wife and child."

He swallowed against the blade. "Okay, okay. His name is—"

But the sound of a motorbike thundering into the parking garage stopped him. Johnson's gaze flashed toward the sound. So did Omair's. Tires squealed as the bike roared around the corner, past them.

Omair ducked quickly behind a post as a soft *thwock* sounded. The bike roared off. Johnson's eyes went white and wide. His body spasmed, and a small, dark hole in the middle of his forehead started to ooze.

Omair watched from the shadows as Travis Johnson's body slid to the ground, taking his secrets and a possible link to the New Moor with him. Omair and Faith might have won this battle—and found love in the process— but the war against the Al Arif family was not yet over.

* * * * *

Don't miss Tariq's story,
SURGEON SHEIK'S RESCUE,
the next thrilling installment of
Loreth Anne White's new miniseries,
SAHARA KINGS.
Available September 2012,
wherever Harlequin books are sold.

REQUEST YOUR FREE BOOKS!
2 FREE NOVELS PLUS 2 FREE GIFTS!

ROMANTIC

SUSPENSE

Sparked by Danger, Fueled by Passion.

YES! Please send me 2 FREE Harlequin® Romantic Suspense novels and my 2 FREE gifts (gifts are worth about $10). After receiving them, if I don't wish to receive any more books, I can return the shipping statement marked "cancel." If I don't cancel, I will receive 4 brand-new novels every month and be billed just $4.49 per book in the U.S. or $5.24 per book in Canada. That's a saving of at least 14% off the cover price! It's quite a bargain! Shipping and handling is just 50¢ per book in the U.S. and 75¢ per book in Canada.* I understand that accepting the 2 free books and gifts places me under no obligation to buy anything. I can always return a shipment and cancel at any time. Even if I never buy another book, the two free books and gifts are mine to keep forever.

240/340 HDN FEFR

Name _____ (PLEASE PRINT)

Address _____ Apt. #

City _____ State/Prov. _____ Zip/Postal Code

Signature (if under 18, a parent or guardian must sign)

Mail to the **Reader Service:**
IN U.S.A.: P.O. Box 1867, Buffalo, NY 14240-1867
IN CANADA: P.O. Box 609, Fort Erie, Ontario L2A 5X3

Not valid for current subscribers to Harlequin Romantic Suspense books.

Want to try two free books from another line?
Call 1-800-873-8635 or visit www.ReaderService.com.

* Terms and prices subject to change without notice. Prices do not include applicable taxes. Sales tax applicable in N.Y. Canadian residents will be charged applicable taxes. Offer not valid in Quebec. This offer is limited to one order per household. All orders subject to credit approval. Credit or debit balances in a customer's account(s) may be offset by any other outstanding balance owed by or to the customer. Please allow 4 to 6 weeks for delivery. Offer available while quantities last.

Your Privacy—The Reader Service is committed to protecting your privacy. Our Privacy Policy is available online at www.ReaderService.com or upon request from the Reader Service.

We make a portion of our mailing list available to reputable third parties that offer products we believe may interest you. If you prefer that we not exchange your name with third parties, or if you wish to clarify or modify your communication preferences, please visit us at www.ReaderService.com/consumerschoice or write to us at Reader Service Preference Service, P.O. Box 9062, Buffalo, NY 14269. Include your complete name and address.

HRS11B

*Harlequin Intrigue® presents a new installment
in* USA TODAY *bestselling author
Delores Fossen's miniseries*
THE LAWMEN OF SILVER CREEK RANCH.

Enjoy a sneak peek at KADE.

Kade saw it then. The clear bassinet on rollers, the kind
they used in the hospital nursery.

He walked closer and looked inside. There was a baby,
and it was likely a girl, since there was a pink blanket snug-
gled around her. There was also a little pink stretchy cap on
her head. She was asleep, but her mouth was puckered as if
sucking a bottle.

"What does the baby have to do with this?" Kade asked.

"Everything. Two days ago someone abandoned her in the
E.R. waiting room," the doctor explained. "The person left
her in an infant carrier next to one of the chairs. We don't
know who did that, because we don't have security cameras."

Kade was finally able to release the breath he'd been
holding. So this was job related. They'd called him in because he was an FBI agent.

But he immediately rethought that.

"An abandoned baby isn't a federal case," Kade clarified,
though Grayson already knew that. Kade reached down and
brushed his index finger over a tiny dark curl that peeked
out from beneath the cap. "You think she was kidnapped or
something?"

When neither the doctor nor Grayson answered, Kade
looked back at them. The anger began to boil through him.
"Did someone hurt her?"

"No," the doctor quickly answered. "There wasn't a
scratch on her. She's perfectly healthy as far as I can tell."

The anger went as quickly as it had come. Kade had handled the worst of cases, but the one thing he couldn't stomach was anyone harming a child.

"I called Grayson as soon as she was found," the doctor went on. "There were no Amber Alerts, no reports of missing newborns. There wasn't a note in her carrier, only a bottle that had no prints, no fibers or anything else to distinguish it."

Kade lifted his hands palms up. "That's a lot of no's. What do you know about her?" Because he was sure this was leading somewhere.

Dr. Mickelson glanced at the baby. "We know she's about three or four days old, which means she was abandoned either the day she was born or shortly after. She's slightly underweight, barely five pounds, but there was no hospital bracelet. We had no other way to identify her, so we ran a DNA test." His explanation stopped cold, and his attention came back to Kade.

So did Grayson's. "Kade, she's yours."

How does Kade react when he finds out the baby is his?

Find out in KADE.
Available this July wherever books are sold.

Copyright © 2012 by Delores Fossen

HIEXP0712

Harlequin

INTRIGUE

CELEBRATE

DEBRA WEBB'S

50TH COLBY TITLE WITH A SPECIAL BONUS SHORT STORY!

Colby Roundup, the story of one woman's determination to remember her past before time runs out, marks Debra Webb's 50th Colby title, and to celebrate Harlequin Intrigue® is giving you a special BONUS Colby companion short story included with this book!

The excitement begins July 2 wherever books are sold!